AMBITION

THE CHARITY DEACON INVESTIGATIONS BOOK 3

P. A. WILSON

FREE EBOOK

Claim your copy of Buying Into Death when you use the QR code to sign up for my newsletter and follow Charity as she solves her fastest case yet!

ONE

I watched as Jake strode across the street and held a gun to the head of a man dressed in black leathers. Just as he reached for the biker's collar, the director shouted, "Cut." Everyone on the set started moving around. Jake rolled his shoulders to relieve the tension of his role before coming back to our side of the street for notes.

He winked at me as he passed. "I told you it might be boring, Charity."

He had no idea how much fun I was having. It might be boring for him. Acting was his job, after all. He would be just as interested if he joined me on a stakeout. At least, that's what I told myself.

Now that Jake and I had found a balance in our relationship – okay, maybe I should say, now that I had learned how to be the happy girlfriend rather than the bitchy one – I could relax and just watch him act. Also, kind of sexy to know that my boyfriend could act the bad-ass but was really a caring guy.

We were filming in New Westminster, the oldest suburb of Metro Vancouver. Down on Front Street, where studios filmed everything from 1940s noir remakes to post-apocalyptic thrillers. Cool and shady, a scent of the working river mixed with the bitterness of diesel from the trains and trucks.

Before I could decide whether to get a snack or go for a walk, wailing sirens caught my attention. A few blocks away three cop cars pulled up in front of what I had assumed was another abandoned storefront. As I watched, the cops entered the building hands on guns. I slipped out of the chair and strolled toward the action.

If there was one thing I found more interesting than watching good looking people act, it was solving crimes, which is why I finally decided to be a private investigator when I grew up. Or, at least, a year ago, I'm not sure I'm grown up yet.

Incoherent shouting drifted down toward me. I heard a woman's voice and then at least two men. I'd heard a few arrests, so I knew that the yelling was an intimidation tactic.

As I listened, wondering what to do, I heard, "Freeze!" Only one word, but what worried me was the escalation in the tone from argument to orders. I had this feeling a witness was needed to keep someone from getting killed.

The woman's voice lost the edge of panic. I could make out the words now that I was closer to the door.

"I didn't do anything."

I knew that voice. It was one I hadn't expected to hear again. One that raised a complicated mix of happiness and annoyance. Val sounded as determined as ever to get her way.

"Put your hands behind your head."

"I called you," she said, anger or frustration sharpening her tone.

"That's fine, now put your hands behind your head." The cop's voice remained calm.

"Look, I didn't kill him. You need to stop hassling me and do your job." Val was mad. The click of handcuffs cut off the next words.

One of the cops escorted Val through the door.

She hadn't changed much in the year since I'd seen her. The hooker clothes had been replaced with a pair of cargo pants and a pale gray tee shirt with a logo too small for me to read. Her hair was bleached and pulled into a tight ponytail, and she looked about ten pounds too thin. The street-smart veneer was still in place as she looked up and met my eyes. A flash of rage before she recognized me. "Charity, what are you doing here?"

She said it as if we'd met in a store. No indication of the situation she was in. She didn't ask for help, but then again, she'd hated having to ask last time. "Hey, Val, what's up?" I tried to match her tone, light and unconcerned, but resentment of how she'd left last time burned.

"Ma'am, please clear the way." The cop shoved Val past me and reached to open the cruiser door.

"What happened?" I wasn't going to let Val disappear again without getting some explanation. "Officer, why is Ms. Wei in cuffs?" I ignored the grin on Val's face. She was in trouble, and acting the smart ass wasn't going to help.

The cop took another step. "Please move away."

I pretended I wasn't intimidated by stiffening my back and standing firm. "I need to know what is happening with Ms. Wei."

"Are you a lawyer?"

"No, but you have her in cuffs, so I assume you aren't just taking her in for questioning."

The cop firmed his lips and gave Val a shove toward the car. He wasn't going to respond.

Val twisted in his grip. "My client was murdered, Charity. They think I did it."

The cop put his hand on Val's head and forced her into the back of the cruiser.

"Is she under arrest?"

He looked at me with narrowed eyes. "No."

He wasn't obligated to tell me anything, let alone the truth. Despite his denial, I could see that Val was going to need representation. "Then she doesn't have to go with you."

"You can tell that to her lawyer."

Val stared at me through the window, the sass and hardness vanished with the slam of the door. The sudden look of fear in her eyes reminding me she was still a teenager. "Val, don't say anything. And don't make the situation any worse. I'll get you a lawyer." I turned back to the cop. "Where are you taking her?"

"The station is on Columbia and 6th. If you get her a lawyer, they'll know what to do." He walked around to the driver's door, got in, and drove away. Val didn't turn to look at me.

I pulled out my phone and then realized that before I found Val some legal help, I needed to know more about what had happened. I looked at the doorway they'd come through. I wasn't hopeful, but, maybe, I could get something before the other cops sent me away.

Stepping quietly across the threshold, I noticed it was some kind of office. Two desks in the open area, a small closed off cubicle and the door to the washroom in the back. No back door. In this part of New West, the back of the building was often bedrock. This didn't look private enough for Val to service a client. I didn't have much hope that she'd found a new way to make money.

One of the remaining cops held up his hand to stop me. "Ma'am, you need to step back outside."

I didn't move, and he wasn't ready to force it. "What happened?"

"Do you know Mr. Schell?"

The other cop put down his radio and moved toward me. "Your name?"

"No, I just... Oh dear." I saw a body in the corner propped into a sitting position. The blood on his chest and the angle of his head confirmed that he wasn't in need of medical attention. I'd seen this kind of thing before, but maybe playing the innocent bystander would get me some sympathy information.

The younger of the two cops walked toward me with his hands spread, like he couldn't decide if he was going to have to catch me as I fainted, or herd me out onto the street. I turned and left before he could get to me.

I put a block between me and the crime scene before I called Lu. "Val's going to be arrested for murder. Can you get her a lawyer?" There was no doubt in my mind that she hadn't done this. The problem was that the cops couldn't risk letting a viable suspect go free. They had to worry about the eventual trial. I only needed to get Val free, which gave me more opportunities.

TWO

The next afternoon I sat with Lu in the waiting room of the New West police station. She was my best friend and, despite the fact she didn't really trust Val that much, she'd come to the rescue, sending a lawyer, and paying the bail.

"She's in my custody," Lu reminded me. "She is going have to stay with Matthieu and me until you clear her."

I hoped it would be a matter of hours rather than days. Val could be hard to live with. "Let's just get her side of the story."

Lu looked at me, a frown crossing her face. "How will her side of the story help? Where's her sister? Weren't they both supposed to be leaving the street life? I don't like what she did last time, when she disappeared. How can you trust her?"

Val had come into my life when I agreed to help find her sister. Both of them had been working the streets, both of them teenagers. I thought I was done with defending her a year ago. "How can I just leave her to deal with this alone?"

Lu pursed her lips. "Fine, but don't let her do that again — leave you without a decent goodbye."

I told her that I'd be careful, that I wouldn't expect anything from Val, and that I'd remember how hurt I'd been, no was.

"Okay, but Matthieu should hear this too. I asked him to join us at home so he can meet our new house mate."

Matthieu was a French ex-cop. He'd helped us find a missing woman last year and fallen in love with Lu. Now they were engaged, and he was my business partner.

Before I could respond, Val stepped through a door behind the reception desk. She looked fragile. The clothes she'd been wearing yesterday were wrinkled, and her hair was tangled rather than tied into a neat ponytail. She looked like she hadn't slept for a week. She glanced at me, then Lu, before coming forward.

A policewoman followed closely. "Ms. Cho?" She looked at Lu who nodded. "Ms. Wei is now in your custody. Do you understand what that means?"

"Yes, my lawyer explained it."

"Well, she's all yours. You'll get a call about a court date." The woman turned and disappeared behind the closing door.

"I guess you think I owe you something for bailing me out," Val said. The old attitude was still in place. I found it oddly comforting.

"A thanks would be in order, Val," I said, annoyed that she hadn't learned to accept help with any grace.

She scowled. "Yeah, well, I didn't ask for the bail money. I didn't do anything, so I could have just got a legal aid lawyer and—"

I interrupted what was turning into a tirade of ingratitude. "Val, stop it. We get that you're scared."

"I'm not scared. I'm mad." Val moved past me. "I'm a legit businesswoman now. And you won't be out your money. I'm not skipping on the bail. I'm going to find out who killed my client, and then you'll get the money back. And I'll pay you back for the lawyer."

I took her arm and stopped her from leaving. "Val, you're in Lu's custody. I'll find out who did this."

She pulled away. "No. I need to do it."

Behind the anger, I heard the tears of a frightened young girl.

We took a quick stop at Val's place, an older building in Uptown New Westminster, where she packed a small bag. Val got into Lu's car with a huff that would have been obvious a block away. How she managed to run a business while still maintaining the teenage attitude was beyond me. I retrieved my car from the parking lot and headed over to Lu's home.

WHEN I WALKED through the front door, I heard arguing coming from the kitchen, so I marched in to try to stop it. "What's the problem now?"

Val turned to me. "They narced on you to Jake. He's on his way over."

"Why is he coming over?" I'd hashed it out with him last night. He wasn't happy about it, but he knew Val was important to me, even if he didn't understand why – I didn't really understand it myself.

Lu poured a glass of white wine and slid it across the counter toward me. "Matthieu called him. I had nothing to do with it."

"We are making a plan to sort out this mess, yes?" Matthieu asked. "Then Jake is involved. Murder is a dangerous game. It is important that he know what we are doing."

He had more experience than I did, but that didn't mean I liked him jumping in like that. We'd worked together for long enough that Matthieu knew I liked my independence. "So, you thought you'd just step in and make sure the men worked it out?"

He held up his hands in surrender. "You know me better than that, I hope. I simply thought of it and made the call. Now, let us put this aside and think about a plan."

I took a big sip of the wine to calm down. Matthieu really wasn't the type to take over the case. He probably did just think it would be more efficient to make the call as soon as he thought about it. It was done anyway. At least I had some warning.

I saw the worry on Val's face. "Jake likes you, Val. He'll be fine."

"Yeah, I'm not so sure about the liking me bit. At least this time I'm not staying with you. He'll be happy that I'm here in the Cho mansion."

I grinned. "At least here you get a real room. No camping in my living room."

"There are some perks. So, what are we going to do next? I gotta get back to my business soon."

Good question. Our next steps would have to be quick. "Let's wait for Jake. No point in making plans we'd have to explain when he gets here." If the cops thought they had their killer, there would be no investigation. Or there would be one, but it would be into Val's background, and that wouldn't help her get off the charge.

"Look, I don't want to get between you and Jake. I can find the murderer myself. I'm good at investigations." Val stirred the ice in her glass with the straw.

"You can't go without me or someone to watch out for you." Lu started pulling food out of the fridge. "I'm not planning to run around with you when there are two perfectly good investigators right here."

The doorbell interrupted Val's response.

"I'll get it," I said, needing a chance to find out what Jake was going to say before he got involved. I pulled open the door and leaned forward to kiss him. He pecked my cheek and wrapped his arm around me.

"Don't look so worried." He pulled me into a deeper kiss as soon as the door closed behind him. "That's to remind you that I love you in case it gets difficult in there."

"Thanks for giving Val a chance." I wiggled out of his arms and pulled him into the kitchen. "Okay we're all here, let's get planning."

"Not so fast." Jake nodded to Val. "How's it going?"

"Not bad. Well, there's the murder charge, but other than that..."

They all shared a laugh, and then silence. I broke the awkward moment. "We can look into why someone would want this Mr. Schell dead."

"He was a sweet old guy," Val said. "There's no reason for anyone to kill him."

Matthieu pulled out a notebook. "And yet, he is dead."

"It looks like you're ready to start getting down to the job. Why did you call me?" Jake poured a glass of tonic water and pulled one of the stools up to the counter. "I'm no investigator. Neither is Lu."

I looked at Matthieu. "You called him for a reason."

"You are right. I did not take this book out to start investigating. I thought that since this is in the family, so to speak, we should agree on how to start."

"We start by asking questions." Val reached for the notebook. "That's how we found Emma."

"No. We start by agreeing on some ground rules," I said. "That's what Matthieu means. That helps us make the investigation go smoother." At least that was the theory he'd been trying to get me to accept.

"Could you just hire a PI?" Jake asked. "I know you can

both do a good job for strangers. Isn't it like a doctor? They don't work on their family?"

"It doesn't work that way." I hoped.

Matthieu topped up my glass. "In this case, I think Charity is right. Val needs someone who believes in her to lead this investigation. I'm not certain we will be able to find someone who will do that."

Lu placed a plate of snacks on the counter. "Val, you can be a pain, but I don't think you did this. The question is how do we get the cops to believe that?"

Val snorted. "Thanks, I think."

Jake looked at me. "We're all in so let's make this as safe as we can, and as fast as possible. We all have something to get back to. And I think Val is going to get cabin fever staying out here, so you'll need to figure out how to keep her with you."

"She'll travel with me," Matthieu said.

"No, I'm with Charity."

I rolled my eyes. This was going to be a long haul. "We'll stay together, Val. Look, Matthieu, I think it would be better if I took the lead. You can cover our cases."

He concentrated on his notebook for a second. "Yes. Perhaps that is best if this takes more than one or two days. But, I think, that tomorrow I will bring Val with me. I can take her to the lawyer and ensure we all understand what needs to be done."

I could see she was going to argue. "Val, I'll pick you up from there. I can do a bit of research in the morning."

She brushed her glass away. "Fine, but I'm not hiding while you investigate."

THREE

Val was in Lu and Matthieu's care until the appointment with her lawyer. That meant I was free to do a bit of background digging before I picked her up. Usually when I started a new case, I had a plan. Something that I could use to find the path that would get the case closed. Of course, my usual case wasn't murder. This time, my starting point had to be the cops.

So, I was back in the police station, in an office sitting, across from a detective who looked about a month from retirement. His eyes carried the weight of the world in their depths and his shoulders were rounded with fat and experience. His name was Detective Reynolds.

"Look, I know you want your friend to be innocent, but we have no other suspects." He looked into the bottom of a coffee mug. It was empty, so he put it down on the same ring it had already made on the desk top.

I figured they hadn't looked very hard. In all fairness, if I didn't know Val, I would think the hard-assed looking girl standing over the body was the killer. "I don't want to tell you how to do your job." Of course, that's exactly what I wanted to do.

"Then don't. Take my word for it. The victim didn't have any enemies. Your girl doesn't have any background here. We checked her out and she's spent some time on the street. Got involved in some gang stuff."

I swallowed my first reaction. Everything he'd said was right, but it wasn't the full story. "She helped to bring in the leader of a gang. And being on the street doesn't mean she's a murderer."

"I don't know what to tell you, Ms. Deacon." He looked at his watch. "I think we're done here. I have an appointment."

I didn't budge. "What was her motive?"

"Maybe the guy got grabby and she decided to do more than just say no. Maybe she thought there was some money. We don't need motive when we catch the killer with the weapon in her hands and blood on her clothes."

"So, you think you have this all tied up?" I struggled to think of something I could say that would change his mind and make him look further. Nothing came to me. Maybe if Val had stayed in touch, I would be able to defend her. I know she didn't do it, but so many things could have happened in the last year and a half that made her look guilty. "Your investigation is closed?"

"Not quite. There are a few details we'll need to gather for the court case." He flipped open the file. "Unless you think Ms. Wei will plead guilty and save us a lot of time and effort?"

This kind of attitude made me wonder why I kept trying to find a way to work with the cops. I know Detective Reynolds wasn't a good example of the whole force, but sometimes I think Matthieu and Leigh were the exceptions. Leigh had given me all the help she could on the first case with Val. Despite the fact that she couldn't just arrest the gang members, she'd bent the rules so I could stop them.

"No. I think you'll have to do the work to prove that she did this. I'll let you know what I find. Maybe I can save you the trouble of a real investigation."

He looked up from the file. "You know better than to get in the way of a murder investigation. You could lose your license."

"You said there's no investigation." I didn't much care what he said. I was not going to let Val be trapped in a court case, one that could easily end up with the wrong result.

"I said we were tying up details. That's still an investigation. I wasn't kidding, if you get in my way, I'll take your license."

I stood up. This wasn't getting me anywhere. I wasn't going to let him bully me into saying something stupid. If he wanted to go around in circles, I'd leave him to it. "Thanks for the heads up. I'll be sure to keep my eyes open."

"You tell that young lady that she better not get into any more trouble while she's out." He stood and pointed to the door.

I let him guide me to the street without making any other comments. I couldn't resist waving goodbye as he shut the door.

The lawyer was in downtown Vancouver. That was a forty-minute drive at this time of day, and Val was expecting me in twenty.

I called as soon as I got in the car. When the receptionist finished greeting me with a list of names and 'how may I assist you?' I said, "I need to speak to Val Wei's lawyer please."

"Your name?"

"Charity Deacon." I guess they were protecting her privacy.

"They are still in a meeting. Can I take a message?"

I told her I was going to be late, and she promised to keep Val there until I arrived.

"We don't want her to violate the conditions of her bail on day one," the receptionist added.

I laughed. "Let's hope she doesn't do it at all."

· · ·

I PARKED in Pacific Center and ran into the lawyer's building. It was almost noon. By the time we got back to New West, we wouldn't have much of the afternoon left for investigating. Val had to be back at Lu's by eight pm or be pulled in and sent to jail.

She was waiting in the lawyer's lobby, in a chair, foot bouncing with impatience. "Sorry, I got held up with the detective."

She stood and shrugged into a leather jacket without responding.

"Val, don't worry. We'll deal with this."

She walked through the lobby and held the door until I grabbed it. I followed her to the elevator. "Val what happened?" This silence had to be caused by something. The Val I knew would be demanding we get into action.

"The lawyer said I might have to do time. I didn't do this. I can't go to jail for something I didn't do." The elevator arrived. It was empty.

There was no point in lying. "The cops aren't looking for anyone else," I said. "I think that might be a good thing."

She glanced at me. "How is that good? If they aren't looking, they won't find the real murderer."

"No, but if they aren't looking, they can't stop us from doing it. Let's get lunch and you can tell me what you know?"

"I don't know much, Charity." She stepped through the door as we arrived at the ground floor. Then she turned with the grin I recognized. "Hey, we're a good team though. Maybe when we prove I'm innocent, I can be a partner in your firm. Like Matthieu, but fun."

I laughed. "Matthieu is fun sometimes. Why don't we solve this case first and then we can talk about a partnership? Just..." I swallowed the sudden tightness in my throat. "Just don't disappear when we do. At least say goodbye this time."

A cloud passed across her face. "Yeah, I'm sorry about that. Emma was really scared they would come after her. She made me go." She grabbed my arm and dragged me to the street. "There's a sushi place around the corner. We can talk there."

The restaurant looked full, but we found a seat near the sushi bar as someone paid their bill. I put my tablet on the table and started the audio recording. "Tell me about Mr. Schell."

"You record all your interviews now?"

"It's easier than trying to read my writing later." I cleaned the slivers of wood off my chopsticks before picking up a few strands of the seaweed salad. "Give me some background then we can decide where to start."

"Okay. Mr. Schell was a good guy. I worked in his office for a little while. He did a lot of community work, and he was real proud of the neighborhood. He said New West was like a small town in a big city."

I had to ask, even if I didn't want confirmation that she was back to hooking. "What did you do for him?"

"I organize people in my business. I organized his stuff," she said.

Relieved that she was doing something legal, I said, "What does that mean? Organize people."

She rolled her eyes. "You know, people get too much stuff, or just stick things wherever, and then realize they need it. I help them get organized. That's all."

I remembered her talent with my files, making sense out of chaos. "So, he had no enemies, no hassles?"

"There was one customer who was pissed that the cruise he wanted was full. A developer kept calling, but I don't know if he was talking about selling."

Not much help. "What about the employees? Anyone disgruntled?"

"Not as far as I could see. I should check to make sure they're okay."

I picked at the sashimi plate. "Maybe they'll know something. Did he have any family?" Family members were sometimes the victim's worst enemies.

"No. You think someone was trying to get some inheritance. I don't think he had any money."

"There must be some motive, Val. Are you sure he was such a nice guy? Everyone has something they don't want to come into the daylight."

"Yeah, he was that nice," she said. "Yeah, I didn't believe it at first. When I was... doing what I did before, there were a few guys that seemed nice until they got you alone. Mr. Schell never made me feel like I was about to be propositioned."

It was the same for every question I asked. The victim was a paragon of virtue. Val didn't seem to realize she was just reinforcing the idea that there were no other suspects. Without a motive, the person who finds the body is the most likely killer.

We left the restaurant and Val said she knew some people we could talk to about Mr. Schell. "He was good with the street people, too. They might have seen something I didn't notice."

She spent the travel time calling people, but either they didn't answer, or they didn't have any information. I found a vacant spot at a meter on Columbia Street. As we stepped out of the car, she jammed her phone into her pocket without saying anything.

She started to walk down the hill to Front Street when a woman came out of a developer's office and called her name. The woman was lean in the way super models were lean. With good cheekbones and lots of chocolate brown hair, she stayed just on the right side of skeletal. "Val, is this true?" she asked in a soft voice.

Val stopped at the sound of her name. I saw her shoulders

tighten and almost heard her count to ten before turning around. "Ms. Whitehall."

"I told you to call me Penelope." The words sounded tired. "Is this true about Mr. Schell?"

"What about him?" The fact that Val didn't like this woman was evident to anyone noticing Val's scowling face, and belligerent stance. Why she felt that way was a mystery I'd get into when we were alone.

I stepped forward before the conversation could go further. "I'm Charity Deacon, a friend of Val's. Can I ask what you know about Mr. Schell?"

She met my gaze and I immediately understood Val's feelings toward her. It was like looking into the eyes of a snake. There was nothing warm in there.

"I understand he's been murdered. What is your business here?" She looked me over like I was shop damaged merchandise.

I kept my cool. "I'm helping to investigate the case."

Val took a few steps toward me and stopped behind Penelope. She grimaced and pointed to her watch. I ignored her and watched the woman analyze what I'd said.

Penelope's eyes warmed as a smile grew on her face. "I'm glad you're helping. It's sad and a bit frightening to have such a... community minded man murdered. Are you working with the police?"

"I'm adding to their efforts. Do you know anything about his background?" Out of the corner of my eye, I saw Val shake her head slightly. I looked at Penelope, hoping Val would get the message and stop distracting me. If we were going to find the killer, we'd need to talk to people she didn't like.

"I only met him recently. I have no idea who might want him dead. I hear that the police have a strong suspect."

"Yes, but there's always unanswered questions." I glanced at the developer's office. "Do you work there?"

"I own Heritage Developers." She checked her watch. "I have to meet someone in a few minutes. If I can be of any help, please let me know." She turned to wave at Val, a little finger wiggle that in a child would be cute, in an adult was like a sneer. Bringing her attention back to me, she asked, "Do you know who will inherit the building where his office was located?"

"Mr. Schell owned the building?" That was interesting.

"Yes, I talked to him about selling. He was considering it. I just wondered if there might be a motive in the inheritance. Some people will do anything to get their hands on money they didn't earn."

She was right, but I didn't want to get focused on any one avenue this early in the investigation. Matthieu had taught me to keep my options open. "We haven't followed that line of investigation yet."

Val was practically dancing to get my attention. "Can I check with you later? In case you think of something else?"

Penelope smiled again, this time her eyes stayed cold. "I'm sure I won't think of anything, but feel free to drop in. I'll let you get back to your investigation."

I couldn't think of any questions to ask so she would stay. "Thanks for your help." I tried to sound like I meant it.

She frowned for a moment and then nodded. "Yes. I'm sorry I don't have more time. Listen, I think you might like our new apartments. I would love to show you some of our floor plans. You seem like the kind of buyer we're trying to attract."

I watched her walk back into the building as though she was headed there when we met. She was cool and elegant, and there was something off about her.

"The ice queen," Val said. "She's trying to buy up the properties on Front Street, and some people are taking the money as fast as she offers. I'm pretty sure she's trying to move the street people away from the warmest places."

Val's history on the streets must make it difficult to deal with the way people treated the homeless. "I imagine she's made a few enemies. It's not easy to try to develop an area." I nodded downhill. "Let's talk to the people you know. Maybe we'll get lucky."

"Maybe the ice queen is the killer?"

"You don't have to sound so hopeful. Just because you don't like her, doesn't mean she's a killer."

We turned the corner. The temperature dropped by about five degrees, and the humidity rose to uncomfortable. The street was shadowed by the parking lot above. It had great atmosphere for movies, but a little creepy in real life.

We looked into the crime scene through the window. The office was taped off and a there was a big seal on the door. The only difference from the last time I'd seen it was the body no longer occupied the far corner.

"Val, what about these people you mentioned?"

She looked over her shoulder. "I guess they're staying away. I should have thought of that. They don't like cops."

"Okay, what about Mr. Schell's friends?"

"If I could get inside, I could find the numbers." She touched the seal. "You think we can break this?"

I pulled her hand away. I wasn't ready to antagonize the cops just yet. "Let's start with the neighbors. Maybe they knew him. Then we'll head back to Lu's and figure out our next steps."

"But I don't want to go back to jail." The fear in her voice was heartbreaking.

"You won't. Unless you break your bail, you're free until trial. That could be months away. Don't worry, we'll figure it out long before things get that far."

We didn't get any information from the neighboring businesses. The two that were still open were new to the neighborhood. They only knew the victim enough to say he was a nice guy, that's what they said about serial killers too.

Val made me walk the length of the street. It was only ten blocks, but there were lots of spaces where someone could hide. She finally agreed that we should leave when we had investigated every doorway and shadowed space and found no one.

"We can come back tonight, right?"

I shook my head. "Nope, you're supposed to stay in the house at night. I'll figure something out. Tomorrow, you and Matthieu can do some research while I start some serious door-to-door work."

FOUR

It turned out that Val had to meet with her lawyer in the morning to sign some final documents, so Matthieu stuck with her while I went back to New West. The lack of information was bugging me. It felt like people were holding back because I was an outsider. The only other possibility was that Val's presence was putting people off. Now I had an opportunity to test both suspicions. Val wasn't with me, and if any of the film crew members were residents, they did know me. There didn't seem to be a person in the industry who didn't love to gossip. So, if there was anything to know, there was a good chance I would hear it on set.

It was a waste of a morning and I had to admit maybe there wasn't anything to learn. I got plenty of gossip, but no information.

I gave up trying to raise a discussion with the makeup girl and went to join Jake who was reading his script notes in the shade of the theater awning. Well, I say theater, it probably had been at some point, but I don't recall hearing coming attractions for a movie called *Lap Dances Half Price*.

Jake kissed my cheek and offered me a bottle of water. "Hi, nice of you to drop by."

"You were busy being a superstar."

He grunted and waved his script. "Superstars need great scripts. This one keeps changing every day. Anyway, did you learn anything?"

I pulled the notebook out of my jacket pocket and flipped through the three pages of notes I'd made. "Well, here's a gem. Did you know that Raymond Burr was from here? You know, Perry Mason?"

"Yes, I did. How does that help your investigation?"

I grimaced. "It doesn't but I thought I should take some notes so people wouldn't think I was wasting their time."

He took the notebook from me and scanned the pages. "You didn't get anything helpful?"

"No, but I've got all afternoon to keep asking." I tried to sound enthusiastic. I'm not sure it worked.

He shook his head. "Sorry, Charity, the director asked me to get you to stop bothering people. You can't ask any more questions."

Crap. "Can you ask questions?" I heard the hustle of noise that meant they were getting ready to shoot again.

Jake looked over my shoulder. "If you didn't get information, I won't get any. I think your answers lie outside the crew."

It looked like I was going to have to do some door-to-door research. It would be difficult to keep a low profile while I did that. I hoped Matthieu and Val were having better luck. I pulled out my phone to call for an update and looked for a quiet place away from the set where I wouldn't interfere with the shoot. As I did, I saw Val slip into a tattoo shop called Ink & Needles, a block away. Dropping my phone back into my purse, I started moving to catch her before the cops found her away from adult supervision.

The door had a cowbell hanging from a nail driven into the frame. It gave a dull clunk as I pushed it open. Val was leaning against the counter flipping through a binder filled with tattoo designs.

"Do you want to go back to jail?" I couldn't let her just do as she pleased. She didn't seem to recognize that her acts had repercussions, despite the fact she'd been taking care of herself as long as I'd known her.

"Chill, I'm fine. How is your part of the investigation? Found any clues, yet?"

I held my tongue. If Val had slipped her bail, Lu would be out more money than either of us could pay back in our lifetimes.

Val must have seen the anger on my face, because she laughed. "Charity, you should be more trusting. You're the one who said I should work with Matthieu."

I looked around, but there was no sign of Matthieu. "I thought that would mean looking up records online, not picking out some new ink."

"If you wanted to keep me away from the street, you should have been more specific." She flipped a page. "Hey, what about this one? It would look cool right here." She pointed to her neck. The tattoo was a stylize dog collar.

"I don't think it will suit you."

She laughed. "What about you? Hey, this one." I looked at the new picture. It was a dragon, red flames pouring from its mouth, blue and yellow scales picked out with black outlines.

The thought of letting someone stick a needle into my skin for an hour or more made me grimace. "Why that one?"

"Because you solved that gang case. You could get a new tat to represent each of your big cases."

I shuddered. "No thanks. So, what kind of research are you doing?" I postponed the discussion about her escape from

Matthieu's custody until we could all point out her folly. Although I should text Matthieu to let him know I had her.

Matthieu stepped out from behind a curtain. "Ah, Charity, you got my message, yes?"

Relief that Val hadn't slipped away was flavored with guilt that I had automatically assumed she was in the wrong. I checked my phone and sure enough there was a text. I'd turned off my phone because that was the rule when the crew were filming. I hadn't bothered to check when I turned it on before coming into the shop. "Okay, so what are you doing here?"

Val grinned at me as if she knew I was trying to cover for my lack of faith.

Matthieu turned as a heavily tattooed woman joined us. "Ah, Angelique, thank you for your help. I will certainly recommend you to my friends who wish to have body art."

"No problem, Matt. I promise I'll find that invitation, I wish I could remember the address. I don't know why it got misplaced. Let me know if you change your mind about the ink. A bumblebee, or maybe a *fleur-de-lis,* would look great."

He smiled before answering, "It is not my decision, Angelique. I fear such a commitment requires discussion with my fiancée." He nodded to Val. "Let us bring Charity up to date."

We sat at the coffee shop next door and I waited to hear whatever they'd found.

"So, are you going to apologize?" Val raised an eyebrow. "Don't pretend you weren't thinking I'd escaped custody. I saw it all over your face."

"Yes, I apologize, but you can't blame me. You have a history of doing as you please."

"Apology accepted." She sipped her latte. "Did you have any luck?"

Matthieu just sat back and let Val run the conversation. I

wondered at his change of attitude. He seemed to be on her side. "I couldn't get anything from the crew, and I was just starting on the stores when I saw you. What's this mysterious invitation?"

Matthieu took out his notebook, a holdover from his years as a gendarme. I'd picked up the habit and it came in handy because people seemed to open up more when I took notes instead of just recording.

He flipped through a few pages before saying, "We did some research online about the real estate holdings. It seems Mr. Schell owned a lot of the property around here at one time or another. Angelique has some old records that may be of interest as well as this mysterious invitation. We shall see."

"What do we know about Angelique?" We needed to make sure we didn't ignore other possible suspects just because Val was convinced of Penelope's guilt.

Matthieu smiled. "I have done some preliminary investigation on our tattoo artist the old-fashioned way. I asked her some questions. She is new to the area. She purchased the tattoo parlor from the previous owner. I need to look into the financial details."

Val sighed pouring frustration and impatience into the sound. "Why are we wasting time with her? We should be focused on Penelope Whitehall."

I let Matthieu explain about keeping an open mind. Maybe she'd listen to him. Whether she agreed or not, she stopped trying to talk us out of investigating Angelique.

"Will you follow up on any other leads? Or do you have anything for me to deal with?" I was feeling a bit of an amateur.

"I must return to the Chapman file." Matthieu reminded me that we still had clients to service.

"Okay. Maybe Val can search for more clues online."

She sat forward as soon as I started talking. "Nope. I am not going to sit at a computer. I'm coming to help you."

I didn't like the idea of Val hanging out where the cops could decide she was harassing people. "You are going to find more information through Google than we will going door-to-door. Besides, I have a feeling it won't take much for the police to put you back in jail."

"They can't do anything to me for just asking questions. And the great thing about Google is the hours. They're open twenty-four seven. I can do research at night."

Matthieu didn't help my argument by nodding.

Annoyed, I asked, "Are you agreeing with Val?"

"Charity, you can't expect her to sit by and wait for you to rescue her. I understand she was helpful in the gang case."

"Yes, but she's not good at keeping a low profile." I didn't need her antagonizing people when I was trying to get information.

"Hey," Val said. "Did you think I'd left? Don't talk about me when I'm right here."

I looked at her. I know part of my problem was her age. Despite her attempts to seem grown up, and despite the fact that she was supporting herself, she was still a kid. The biggest part of my problem was her inability to let people be assholes. If she had to fight back every time someone said something she didn't like, it would turn off any flow of information. But Matthieu was right. She'd helped me shut down that gang. And I wasn't getting anywhere going it alone.

I gave up trying to fight the inevitable. "You need to let me take the lead and you need to keep your opinions to yourself until we're alone. Okay?"

"Whatever you need. The sooner we solve this, the sooner I get back to my business."

"I have an idea." I stopped Val's charge into a bookstore by grabbing her jacket. "Do you have an office?"

She laughed. "No. I work out of my apartment, like most people do these days. Why?"

"I thought we could start with your client list. It would give us a warm opening. That is, if they're all local."

"Hey, that's a great idea." She dug for her phone. "Just don't tell them I'm a suspect, okay? I don't think that will be good for business. Okay, here's my contact list."

I looked at the screen she held up to me. There were a lot of names on the list. "These are all your clients? How do you have time to get them all organized?"

"They aren't all current. I'm working with four people right now. The rest are either old clients, or some people who aren't ready yet." She frowned at me. "Did you think I was just playing at business?"

"No. I know you better than that." I looked at the list again. "Did you get Mr. Schell's business through referral?"

"Yes. Mrs. Irons made the connection."

"Let's see if we can talk to her first." I waited while Val made the call. She was professional and friendly on the phone. Mrs. Irons agreed to meet with us right away.

Her building was only three blocks away. Unfortunately, like most of New Westminster, it was three blocks uphill. I had to take a moment to catch my breath before Val buzzed the apartment. She just laughed at me.

When we reached the apartment door, a sweet old lady was waiting for us. She must have been about ninety; a cloud of pink tinged white hair framed her face. Her eyes, which might have been deep blue when she was younger, were faded almost to grey. "Welcome, would you like a cup of tea?"

I followed them into the apartment, agreeing to tea, although the heat was on and I didn't relish a hot drink. "It's nice to meet you."

"You want to ask questions about that murder. Well, let's

wait until the tea is ready." She pottered into the kitchen and I heard china rattling.

She came out with a tray holding cups and a bag of cookies. Val jumped up and took the tray. Mrs. Irons settled into the armchair. "Now, I want to be clear, I don't think Val had anything to do with it. I told that policeman he was barking up the wrong tree, but he didn't want to listen to me. What can I do to help?"

Val waved her hand at me to lead the questions. "We don't know that much about Mr. Schell. You referred him to Val. Were you friends?"

She dipped a chocolate covered cookie into her tea before answering. I could almost see the wheels working in her mind while she stalled. "I can't say we were friends. I knew him from the Chamber of Commerce. He was struggling with his records. Something about an audit coming and he was disorganized. I told him about Val helping me so much."

"Did you know anything about his private life?"

She blushed. "No. I don't know much about that kind of thing."

I looked at Val. She shrugged.

"What kind of thing?" I asked.

She reddened further. "Oh, that sex club stuff. I know I shouldn't be such a prude, but I don't understand why someone needs to be tied up to enjoy sex. Well, I say tied up, but I'm sure there's more to it than that."

"Mr. Schell?" Val's words burst out before I could ask anything else.

"Oh, yes dear. There was a club. I suppose there still is one. They operate out of the basement of Doomsday, that old night-club on Columbia Street."

The one the film crew had been using as a backdrop? "We'll look into that. Perhaps the killer came from that part of his life."

I sipped the tea, which was so strong I could feel my teeth turning yellow. "Is there anything else we should know about him?"

"I can't think of anything, but I'm sure his death is going to be part of the gossip at the poker club tonight. I'll phone you if I hear anything helpful." She took another cookie.

Val reached over and patted the old woman's hand. "Don't get yourself into trouble, Mrs. Irons. Maybe we should come to the club and ask some questions."

"No, dear, no one will talk if there are strangers around. Don't worry, I'll be careful." She smiled at us over the brim of her cup.

I didn't argue. She was probably looking forward to leading the gossip about the investigation. I gave her a few questions to ask, hoping she'd get us some information. If she didn't get anything, I could follow up.

"I did hear something about that development," she continued after writing the questions down.

"Which development?" I asked, glaring at Val who had leaned forward and seemed ready to jump into the discussion.

"Oh, you know, that one where they let the facade collapse by mistake." She raised an eyebrow. "Well, they say mistake, but you know how it is, they'll do anything to save a few dollars."

Val finished her tea. "What did you hear? Was it about that Penelope woman?"

I knew she was convinced that Penelope was the killer, but it couldn't be that easy. Just because she was unlikeable, didn't make her a killer. I didn't say anything because Mrs. Irons might have a real clue.

"Oh, no dear, it's about that councilman. The rumor is he's in the developer's pockets. It's truly shocking how corrupt people can become when they have a little power."

So, it was nothing helpful, just the usual accusations around unpopular development approvals. I finished the tea and made excuses. I needed to get into some cool air before I passed out.

In the elevator, I turned to Val. "She's a character."

"Yeah. Her daughter brought me in to help. Before I worked with her, she was ass deep in tchotchkes. They were going to put her in a home. I helped her clear out the stuff, and she seemed to come back to her senses as the room got tidy. What about Mr. Schell?"

"I think this sex club thing has a lot of potential to find an alternate suspect. Maybe he was going to blackmail someone, and it backfired. If we can find anything that points to another motive, the cops will be off your back." I hoped my optimism would be rewarded.

"Yeah, but we need to find out who killed him, right? Getting me off the hook is number one, but we need to solve his murder."

I nodded. "Yes, but don't tell the cops that, they won't like us digging into an ongoing investigation. And if they have another suspect, there really will be an official investigation."

FIVE

The crew was still filming outside the nightclub, and I didn't think I would get away with slipping inside until they were done. I promised Val we'd check with Jake before I left to find out the schedule. If they were moving locations later, the crowds would go too. Then we could snoop around here without attracting too much attention. In the meantime, we could go back to knocking on doors.

There wasn't much else I could think of doing. "Let's have another look at your list of clients," I said.

Val pulled out her phone and checked. "I don't know if anyone is going to be helpful. It's not like my clients were part of a club or anything." She giggled. "Well, I guess, maybe they are."

I ignored the insinuation. "What if we talked to some of his tenants? Do you have a list of those?" I wish I'd asked Matthieu for details before he took off.

"Yeah. We put it in the cloud. Hang on."

For someone who hated technology a year ago, Matthieu had developed a love of it. One of the best things he'd brought to the business was a drive to make things as easy as possible. The bureaucracy of the *Gendarmerie* tied his hands too often, and now he could see the benefit of using tools when there were no rules.

"Here it is," she said. "Okay, he owned the building that Angelique runs the tattoo shop in and the nightclub – convenient. And a couple of old shops on Front Street. I think those are empty."

Mr. Schell had six tenants in his property, so we started with the first name and worked our way down. Two of the shops were closed because of the filming, and neither had left an emergency number for contact. But the other four owners were happy to chat.

Unfortunately, the tenants in the first three offices, a book-keeper, a notary, and a mani/pedi place, didn't have any information that helped. After two hours of sipping coffee with chatty businesspeople without getting any useful information, I needed a break.

Val seemed to still be optimistic. "Come on, Charity. There's only one left and then we can start on the other neighbors."

Even when we'd prompted, none of the people knew anything about the sex club, or rather, none of them had mentioned it. I had noticed a few bashful looks. I made a note to follow up later with them. It might take a bit of discretion, and that meant no Val. I looked at the address for the last tenant. It was just two doors away. "Let's keep it short. No refreshments, okay."

She nodded. "Yeah, I can't drink any more coffee. But this place might be more interesting anyway. They've just opened."

It was an organic vegan cafe. Looking through the window I could see two pale young women sitting at a table in the corner. The man behind the counter looked earnest and hip. He was wearing dark jeans, red suspenders, and a tartan shirt. I hoped we weren't in for a lecture on the evils of eating anything that tasted good. "Okay, you start talking to him and I'll observe."

She straightened and shot me a look. "Are you planning on training me to be a private investigator?"

I did not need another partner. "No. You're just closer to his age than I am. I think he might relate better."

She smoothed her clothes like she was trying to look more like a detective. "Okay, but I'd be good at it. Maybe you should think about it. I'm persistent, and people like to talk to me."

I didn't think she was serious. If she was, there were a few hard lessons for her to learn about having to talk to people she didn't like, Penelope being the example I'd use. I opened the door and held it while she walked through.

"Good afternoon, can I get you taste of our latest tea blend?" My bladder twinged at the thought of more liquid.

Val marched up to the counter and held out her hand. "Hey. I'm Val Wei. You're kinda new to the neighborhood."

"Bryant Waters." He shook her hand and looked at me with a weak smile.

Val didn't even glance over her shoulder. "She's my assistant. I run a local consulting business. I thought I would drop by and welcome you to the neighborhood."

I tried not to wince at the pushy way she just ignored me. Bryant focused on her, leaving me to watch. He didn't try to push the tea, or the vegan brownies, he just waited for Val to continue. I was grateful, but his business wouldn't last long if he didn't start selling.

"I guess you heard about the murder, right?" she asked. "I just wanted to tell you this isn't a bad area. That's never happened before."

Bryant nodded. "Yes, he was my landlord. We've only been open a month, and now I don't know what's going to happen."

"That's crappy. But if you have a lease, you should be okay."

Val leaned toward Bryant. "I think the estate will take a while to wrap up, since it's murder."

He looked down at the counter. "I should have listened to that developer though. She said it was a bad bet leasing here right now. I just figured the customers would come with the new development. It was a big part of my business plan."

"Like younger people would move in? Yeah, I know. It would help my business too." Val did seem to have a talent for drawing a conversation out. She looked around. "You might want to consider your marketing plan, Bryant. There are a lot of young people already living near here."

Bryant fiddled with the plates of samples. "I thought I had a great deal here. I could cater to the people coming in with the development, and I could take advantage of the low rent on the old spaces."

Val made a sympathetic noise. "It was a good plan. It might still be okay. I don't think anyone will push you out. The new owner will want tenants, right?"

"I think the developer, Penelope, I think she meant that this building would be torn down. I should have listened." He slumped. How he expected to make a success of the business with that attitude I didn't know.

Val patted his arm. "If she meant that, then you still have a while. Until they know who killed him, no one will be looking to hand over any of his stuff."

Bryant straightened, clearly taking heart from Val's words. "I guess. And I could look for another site while I wait." His words were bereft of hope.

"Do you mind if I ask about Mr. Schell?" Val asked. "I mean, maybe you know something the police need to solve the crime. We don't want a murderer running around loose."

Bryant shrugged. "I only met him a couple of times. He seemed okay. Although, he got pissed when I told him about the developer. I think they were trying to pressure him to sell. He went off on a rant about losing the heritage of the neighborhood, and traffic problems. I was kind of surprised. But then he lowered the rent, so I went for it."

Val held out her hand. "Well, I hope it works out for you. I'll drop by for lunch one of these days. It's nice to see something healthy on the street."

"Yeah, I figured vegan was the latest thing and I would get more customers. I figure keeping up with the trends is the way to go, right?" He leaned in close and said, "I don't know how people can live without butter and cheese. Don't tell anyone I said that."

Val laughed. "Our secret."

A few minutes later, I was standing on the corner trying to convince Val to let me see Penelope alone. "Look, it's only for this one interview," I said, hoping it was true. "The important thing is to get the information, if she has any."

Val wasn't interested in the rationality of the argument. "It's me who's the suspect here. I think I should be part of the interview. I'll be good, I promise."

She was right about it being her life, but I was right about the investigation. "Val, you have to trust me. I will get any information she has." And it will be easier without the cheeky sidekick.

"We stuck together last time." Her eyes were filling with tears. "The only time we didn't stick together you got beaten up."

Oh.

"Val, I'll be okay. No one is after me." I swallowed the feeling of... I don't know what it was. "It's different, Val."

I watched her take control of her emotions. Her mouth tightened, and then she wiped her eyes with her fingers. "How do you know that?"

I handed her a tissue. "I know because Matthieu wouldn't have let us do this alone if he thought there was a problem. I trust his instincts. And if anyone is in danger, it's you."

"Why would anyone want to hurt me?" Val was truly surprised. "I don't know anything."

I counted out the reasons on my fingers. "One, the killer doesn't know that. Two, we don't know the motive; it could be about something you might have found when you were working with him. Three, you are the only suspect the police are investigating, if you are dead, maybe the case will be closed. Four—"

Val held up her hands in surrender. "Okay. I get it. But I still don't get why I can't come with you. I can observe."

"Because she doesn't like you, and she wanted to talk to me. Remember I am just the kind of person they are trying to attract." I saw she wasn't convinced, so I brought out the big guns. "Val, what if she gets annoyed enough to call the cops. It would only take one call to have your bail revoked." I looked at my phone for the time. "Go stay with Jake, and I'll be back in a half hour or less. Then we can go home and regroup."

She sighed and then nodded. "Okay. Don't get beaten up."

"I promise. Don't do anything to disrupt the filming."

SIX

I stopped worrying about Val and started worrying about how I would get information out of Penelope without having to listen to her sales pitch. Price aside, I liked living on my floating home, and didn't want to move to New Westminster.

The developer's office was busy. Penelope smiled and held up a finger for me to wait while she finished her conversation. I walked over to the finishings board and checked out the latest in counter tops and cupboard handles. Maybe it was time to do a little renovation. The contrast between the milky-white stone counter top and the dark cabinets was kind of attractive.

"Charity, right?" Penelope interrupted my thoughts. "So glad you came back. Are you looking for a new place?"

"The finishes are great," I said, avoiding her question. "I was wondering if I could talk to you about Mr. Schell."

"The man who was murdered?" She acted like she didn't know him. "Isn't your friend the suspect?"

"I'm trying to learn a bit about him. I don't understand why Val would have committed murder. She's not crazy, so there must be a good reason she's a suspect."

"The police know what they are doing." She pointed to the floor plans. "Did you see our layouts?"

"No. Did you know Mr. Schell? He owned a lot of property around here."

"I did know that, I think. Do you live alone, or would you need a larger unit?"

It was getting hard to ignore the sales pitch. Maybe if I pretended to be interested, she'd be more forthcoming. "When will you be complete?"

She smiled. "Downsizing or up?"

"I'm not sure."

"Well, we'll have occupancy in eight months, so you have time to figure it out."

One of her assistants approached and stood at her elbow. "What do you want, Ken?"

Val was right about the ice queen. The temperature dropped ten degrees as she showed her displeasure at being interrupted.

"I need to discuss an offer," the young man said. "Can we take a few minutes?"

I answered for her, "I can wait. I really wanted to talk about Mr. Schell. So, take your time." The guy paled, glancing at Penelope and then at me. I couldn't tell whether it was fear of Penelope or shock because I mentioned a murder victim. "Really, take your time."

Penelope narrowed her eyes. Then she smiled, and the temperature dropped another few degrees. "Fine. I'll just be a minute with Ken."

I nodded and pretended to study the layout she pointed to. If I were in the market for a new place, I might be tempted. But I wasn't. I picked up a brochure and watched her with Ken. He kept flicking his gaze at me when she was focused on the paperwork. She crossed out a few lines, scribbled something, and then shoved the papers back at Ken.

I put the brochure in my purse and decided the gentle approach wouldn't work. Penelope came back to me and I jumped in. "So, did you know Mr. Schell?"

She raised an eyebrow. I chose to believe it was because she was impressed with my approach. "Yes. I knew him enough to say hello. You're right, we met because he owns property. I know he was helping your friend with the homeless. She's quite a little activist."

"Val is passionate about things." Damn. She was good with distractions. I was going to have to work harder to keep on my topic, not hers.

Penelope sneered. "Yes, that's one way to put it. I don't know anything else about Mr. Schell. Although you might want to check with your friend's buddies on the street. Maybe they heard Mr. Schell was going to sell more properties to me."

"Really? I heard he was against it."

She looked surprised. "He helped me get the permits for this building."

That was easy to check up on, but maybe she was lying on the off chance I wouldn't follow up. "That seems to be the opposite of what people think."

"He didn't want anyone to know. He was well aware that it would be unpopular, at least until we move some new blood into the area and change the attitude. Now, can I set you up with a broker to help you with the financing?"

She wasn't going to say anything else unless I got more than just firm. And I saw a glint of challenge in her eye. If I pushed too hard, she'd push back. She was hiding something, but I didn't know what. Over my couple of years in the business of investigating, I'd had this feeling more than a few times. Sometimes people were hiding important information and sometimes it was nothing – well nothing to do with the case anyway.

I pulled out my phone as if I had a call. "Thanks for your time, Penelope. I'm sure we'll figure this out." I shook her hand and left. I wished I could have connected with Ken, but he was talking to a young couple who looked like they would be great customers for the vegan cafe.

It was getting late, and we'd have to head home soon. If I couldn't get the Ice Queen to give me information, I'd have to take another look at Val's client list. She might not think anyone would be of help, but I'd noticed that New Westminster was a pretty close community. Someone would know something.

WHEN I GOT BACK on the set, Val was waiting for me. The crew was setting up the next shot, so we could talk. I told her what I'd learned.

Val grabbed her coat and started moving toward the office. "Let's go find this Ken guy. Maybe he knows something."

"Hold on. We don't know what he might know. Let's wait until we can get him without Penelope around." I pulled out my notebook. "We probably don't need to head over to Lu's just yet. Let's list who you know in town and see if we can find some kind of connection."

"I told you my clients don't know each other." She pulled out her phone anyway.

"I know you don't think they know Mr. Schell, but, maybe, they know Penelope. If she is trying to develop the town, she might have made some connections." She'd probably made enemies more than connections.

We started listing Val's clients, then her friends. "I only know some of the first names of these guys," she said. "And some of them are probably street names."

I looked at the list, thirty names. "How do you know these people?" I pointed to the list of street names.

"They're homeless. I bring them food, and sometimes I have clothes or blankets."

"So, they won't know Penelope?"

"They might. You'd be surprised what you learn on the street. What's the next step?"

I looked at the list again. There was nothing apparent to connect the people. "Okay, are any of your clients in the construction business? Or somewhere in the development approval process?"

She chewed her lip for a minute. "Okay I —"

"Quiet, please." The words came from the director. We had about thirty seconds to get somewhere we could talk. I didn't want to go to my place, or Lu's, because if we figured out a connection, we needed to follow up on it. And that would be useless if we were that far away from here. I didn't want to disappear on Jake either, but he was across the street getting ready to go on camera.

I grabbed my phone and texted him that we were going to leave, and then pointed Val to Bryant's cafe. "Maybe we should have some tea while we figure this out."

She shrugged. "Sure, but I think we should go find Ken. Maybe let him see us going into the cafe?"

It wasn't a bad idea. If we could talk to Ken without alerting Penelope, it would save a lot of aggravation. "You go to the cafe and I'll see what I can do about getting him there."

"Okay." She looked over her shoulder and frowned.

"What?" I couldn't see anything that would upset her.

"Nothing, just a guy." She started walking to the cafe.

I let it go. She was capable of dealing with any guy on the set. There were no actual dangerous people there, just a few odd types. I told her to order me a tea. Not my favorite drink, but I didn't know how bad the coffee would be at Bryant's, since his heart wasn't in it.

I walked past the cafe as she went in. This time the place was empty. Another bad sign for his business, but it would give us a chance to talk without wondering who was listening in.

A few storefronts over, I looked in the window of the development office. Penelope was nowhere in sight, but neither was Ken. I would have to go inside and hope she wasn't in the back somewhere I couldn't check from outside.

I pushed open the door and glanced around. The space was mostly open, but there was a cubicle and, of course, Penelope's office. I wandered over to the cubicle and heard Ken's voice on the phone.

"I'll make sure I lock up, Ms. Whitehall. Yes. No problem." He ended the call, and then jerked in surprise when he noticed me. "Hello, have you made a decision about buying into the building?"

At least he remembered me. "No. I was hoping to discuss the options with Penelope, is she here?"

"She's left for the day. Can I answer your questions?"

I wasn't convinced she was gone. She struck me as someone who might want to test her employees by dropping in to check that they were working. So, I didn't want to ask my questions here. Besides, Val would kill me if I left her out. "I'm meeting someone for tea. If you have some time, can you join us?"

An expression crossed his face similar to the last time. I couldn't tell if it was fear or concern. Then he smiled. "Of course, I'm happy to answer questions. Just to be clear, you're still Ms. Whitehall's client, though. Where will you be?"

I told him and made to leave, but he called me back.

"I won't be able to close the deal for you," he said. "If you're ready to buy, that is. I don't want her to think I've poached her client."

Penelope had done a good job of instilling fear in Ken. I wondered if it was more than greed. Being willing to lose a sale rather than fight over commission seemed a bit extreme. "I'm still browsing," I said. He smiled and the tension in his face relaxed.

"WELL?" Val asked as soon as I entered the cafe. "Is he coming?"

I shrugged, not sure about the last exchange. "Maybe. Let's try to find a link between your other contacts while we wait."

Bryant gave us some cookies on the house, gluten free vegan ones. I preferred my cookies to be made with butter and eggs, but they weren't bad.

"I've been looking at my client list, Charity." Val passed me a sheet of paper. "I can't see any connections."

I looked over the names. "How do you get new clients?"

"I dropped off flyers, and I ask for referrals. I did a presentation for the Chamber."

She'd been putting a lot of effort into this business. I wasn't surprised. Val was a determined young woman. "I was hoping you had more people refer others. Like Mrs. Irons."

"I was hoping that too, but it's not that easy." She stared at the list. "I do okay, but..."

"You've built a good list of clients pretty fast, Val. It's not like you were building a suspect list."

She laughed. "I guess not. Yeah, I do okay. I manage to pay my bills, and I have enough to feed the street guys."

"You need an alliance. Maybe we can refer business to you." Maybe she wouldn't disappear after this case like she did before.

She grinned. "Thanks. Maybe I can do the same for you."

It was a bit odd that there would be no connection between thirty people who lived in this small town. It wasn't impossible, but odd.

Perhaps the connection wasn't obvious. "Are any of these people in the same building?"

"These two," she said pointing to the names. "But I don't know if there's any other connection. It's not like I do investigations on my clients. I take cash, and I go through their stuff."

She had a point. It made more sense for her clients to do a background check on her. But she was right. There wasn't much need for her to go deep into the life of a new client. "Can you remember finding anything interesting in someone's stuff?"

She sat back and crossed her arms. "I try not to look, or I guess, not pay any more attention than I need to. It's kind of creepy to nose around while I organize." She reached for the list. "I might not have details, but I do know how I categorized things."

She went through the list making notes. "Okay, here's what I did for them. And now you mention it, this guy had a lot of information on guns and poisons."

I read the notes. "Mr. Smith... are you sure that's his name?"

She laughed. "Yes."

Val had categorized the contents of research boxes. The labels were fast death, slow death, and unusual poisons. "How come this didn't make you suspicious while you were doing the work?"

She shrugged. "I guess I didn't put it together as I worked. Like I said, I try not to snoop." She pointed at the list, "That was only a couple of hours work in a week-long project."

I took a picture and sent it to Matthieu for research. I pushed the list back to her and looked at my watch. "I don't think Ken is coming. Let's get back to Lu's now. Maybe Matthieu has something for us."

She stuffed the list of names into her pocket. "Yeah. Maybe."

"Don't be so down. I'll just check in with Jake and we'll go."

SEVEN

The shoot was in one of its frequent holding patterns. There was a small crowd around the craft table, but Jake was nowhere to be seen.

"Do you have to tell him when you leave?" Val tugged my jacket. "Don't you have a mind of your own?"

I turned to tell her that I certainly did have a mind of my own and caught her in mid-chortle. "Very funny. I just need to leave him a note. It's not like we're doing anything that should worry him." I hoped it would stay that way, but I wasn't sure that this case would remain civilized. In fact, we needed it to stop being that way.

Jake's bag was slung over the back of his chair, so I dug around inside until I came up with a notebook. I could have texted him, but who knows when he might be able to check his phone. And I hated tearing pages out of my own notebook.

"Hey," a strange voice broke into my thoughts. I turned to see that the words were addressed to Val. "You're that girl who hangs out with the street people, right?"

I glanced up at her to see if Val needed help, while thinking it was unlikely. A guy, who might have been late teens, or mid-twenties, was lounging against a chair nearby. He had spiked blue hair and was dressed in baggy jeans and a *Game of Thrones* tee shirt. He was probably an inch away from falling on his ass if he pushed the chair any further.

Val straightened a little. "Yeah, what about it?" She crossed her arms. "You have a problem with helping people down on their luck?"

He jerked up and the chair went over in a clatter. His face flushed, and he bent to set the chair upright. "No, uh. I. Uh." He coughed, and I could almost see him telling himself to get it together. "No. Actually I'm a documentary film maker and I wondered if you would be cool and help me make a documentary about them."

"Like that's an original pick up line." Val turned away from him. I watched his face flush a deeper shade.

"No. Oh God, no. I didn't mean anything sleazy." He stepped toward us and then seemed to notice me. "I want to make a movie that brings attention to the problem street people have when they are out in the 'burbs. Like all the services are in the city. Right?"

Val stopped moving away. "Okay Mr. Big filmmaker. What movies have you made?"

He swallowed. "Well, I'm still building my portfolio, okay. This would be my first documentary."

She shrugged. "I don't think it's a good idea. The people I know are proud. They might not want to be in a movie."

He deflated, shoulders slumping. "Will you think about it?"

Val's eyes narrowed. I saw that as my cue to step in before she demolished his ego. There was always a chance that he might get information for us, so I needed to get him feeling helpful. "I'm Charity Deacon." I held out my hand.

He took it and gave a gentle shake. "Rory MacDonald."

"This is Val." She ignored his hand. "So, Rory, we're pretty busy, but maybe you can tell us about your plans."

He brightened. "Like a pitch, yeah?"

I nodded and glared at Val who rolled her eyes but paid attention.

"Okay, cool. Like I said, it's about the homeless people here in the 'burbs. I think they don't get the services they need, right? And I want to make a web doc to get people behind a movement."

He had a long way to go before he'd get any backers, but maybe a web doc didn't need finances. "It sounds interesting. Look we have to go, but why don't you work on your pitch. I'm sure Val might be interested if it helps the street people."

He looked surprised that anyone had actually listened to him. "Okay. You'll be back tomorrow?"

"Yes, we'll be here." The noise around the set started to organize, going from general chatter, to instructions and agreement. There would be a call for silence soon. "You should get back to your job." I nodded toward the clump of technicians.

"Yeah. I'm not with them. I work with the caterer. Well, for now." He grinned. "One day they'll be catering my shoot, yeah?"

I laughed. "Yep, I'm sure that's what's in the cards."

He waved to Val and went back to the craft truck.

Val watched him go. "Why did you encourage him?"

I finished the note and pointed toward the parking lot. "Why not? He might be the next Michael Moore. You should think about his offer. It would be good for the street people to get some services."

She sneered at the idea. "No, what will happen is they'll get moved along. That's the problem. It's never about getting help. It's always about getting them gone."

She probably knew more about it than I did. I remembered

how adamant she'd been that she wasn't homeless when we first met. "You know, I think Rory liked you."

"Yeah, I don't need a boyfriend, Charity." She marched toward my car before I could answer. She was wrong. She needed people around her. A boyfriend wouldn't hurt, at least one like Rory, who was kind of shy and kind of confident. I let it go. There was plenty of time to get them together – maybe after a little background check.

We didn't make it to the car. Before we got to the ramp into the parking lot, two of New Westminster finest intercepted us, flashed their badges, and made us stop. I stepped between the cops and Val, hoping she would keep her smart-ass attitude inside.

"Officers, how can I help you?" I kept my tone even. I didn't want to antagonize them, and I thought that it was going to be easy to get them annoyed, if not outright angry, since they wanted Val to be their killer.

The cop who spoke was as wide as he was tall, blue trench coat hanging open, revealing a barrel chest that seemed to be all muscle. "We've been contacted by Ms. Whitehall regarding harassment charges."

"Who's Ms. Whitehall?" The words were out before I remembered that was Penelope's last name. Before I could correct myself, the cop answered.

"Don't try to play us. She claims you've been interrupting her business with questions about the murder of Mr. Schell."

Val shifted behind me, and I wondered if she'd been poking around when I didn't have my eye on her.

"The developer, right?" I asked, trying to think of a way to get some information out of them.

The cop nodded.

"Have you been questioning her?" The second cop chimed in. This one was younger and wimpier than his partner. They both took a step forward. I tried not to be intimidated. It didn't work well.

I took a step back. "Once. She invited me to talk to her. I don't know why she thinks I've been harassing her." Val put her hand on the small of my back as if to remind me to stay calm. That did work.

The musclebound cop gave one nod then stepped back to give us more room. "She didn't mention the invitation. Maybe she meant that she wanted to talk to you about buying a unit in her new building."

What was it with everyone trying to sell me an apartment in New West? "Maybe."

"Did she, at any time, indicate that she wanted you to leave?"

I thought about the discussion. There was no way I would have missed a clue that she was uncomfortable with my questions, even if I didn't act on the clue. In fact, I couldn't imagine her letting any situation become uncomfortable for her or being too subtle to be understood. She was just being a bitch by contacting the cops. "No, she didn't. Look, I have a place to go. Is she pressing charges? Do I need lawyer?"

There was silence. I couldn't tell if it was a technique to get me to say something incriminating to fill the silence, or if they didn't know what to do. I was tired of hanging out here. "Is she in the habit of getting you to do her bidding?" I knew I should have found a more pleasant way to say it, but I figured it was worth a shot.

The wimpy cop narrowed his eyes. I think he was going for menacing, but it came across as petulant. Other than that, there was no response.

"What do you know about her?" I asked. "Do you just go out and harass people on her orders?" So much for trying not to antagonize them.

"We aren't harassing you." This came from the detective with the muscles. If he was going for reassuring, he needed practice.

Just as I was about to say we were going to leave, Val stepped from behind me and glared at the cops. "Are you guys for real? I mean, is it illegal to talk to someone in public? It's not like we were hunting her down at home. You would be better off spending your time looking for real criminals."

I grabbed her elbow to pull her back behind me, but it was too late. I saw the slight tightening of square cop's jaw. She'd pushed a button. He didn't say anything right away, just held up a hand to keep me from leaving. Then his words came out tightly controlled, "Ms. Wei. Harassment is a serious crime. This time, we'll just give you a warning. I suggest you stay away from Ms. Whitehall and her company."

I hated to outright lie to the police. I wasn't going to back off the investigation, but I guess I could give Penelope some space. "I have some other leads."

"This isn't your investigation, Ms. Deacon." That came from the skinny cop in a sneer of a voice.

"Are you investigating?" I knew the answer.

"We are investigating the murder. We don't need an amateur getting in the way."

"Charity isn't an amateur. She's brought down gangs," Val shouted.

"Val, it's okay." I took her elbow and started to move toward the parking lot. "I don't know if you are looking for anything other than proof that Val is the murderer, but she isn't, and I'll keep investigating until I prove it. Now, if there are no charges, we need to go."

They separated so we could pass between them. As we did, the skinny cop said. "It doesn't sound like you're all that impartial either."

I turned to stare at him. "As you said, I'm an amateur. I don't need to be impartial. But I know Val, and she didn't do this."

He opened his mouth to answer, but his partner elbowed him and he snapped it shut again.

The square cop nodded at me. "Take care as you snoop around. You might run into some dangerous people."

This time he actually sounded like he meant it. I gave a quick smile to reduce the tension. "I've met my share of dangerous people. Don't worry about me."

"I don't want you to be the next body we find." With that he headed back to Columbia Street. His partner gave me stare and then followed.

EIGHT

"I think we need to do some investigating into Penelope," Matthieu voiced what I had been thinking since the cops had stopped us.

We were back at Lu's, and I had just finished telling them about the day. Val had been uncharacteristically quiet while I talked. I could see she was brewing something, a plan, or a question, or more likely, an objection in her mind, but I didn't think it would help to get into it right now.

I nodded toward the laptop on the dinner table. "I didn't think Lu would be happy with you bringing work into the living areas of the house."

"I'm not." She walked in with a tray of snacks. "This is a special case. I don't think house rules should get in the way of doing the job. Besides, we won't all fit in his office."

The more heads in this the better as far as I was concerned. "Where do we start? What about Mr. Smith, Val's client?"

"It took a bit of searching, Smith isn't such a great clue when you want to be sure you have the right one. But the other information you gave me allowed me to narrow it down," Matthieu said.

"To what?" Val asked. "Was I organizing the life of a murderer?"

Matthieu brought up a page on Amazon. It was an author bio. "Val, is this your Mr. Smith?"

She peered at the picture. "Yeah, maybe ten years ago."

"Then he is not a suspect, I think." Matthieu pointed. "He writes crime books. What you mentioned in his collection was his research."

"Great." Val stood and started pacing. "I think we should start asking Penelope The Witch questions. Like she thought we were harassing her, then we should do it."

I understood her frustration, but I also knew, well I'd learned, that barging in wasn't the best way to get what you need. It was the best way to get people to push back, and, maybe, to fight back. "Let's do some research first, Val. And we should also look into Angelique."

"It will just be a waste time. Angelique didn't do anything. She's nice." Val flounced herself into a chair. Was she determined to remind us she was a teenager and not a mature businesswoman?

I ignored the attitude, hoping it would disappear if no one paid attention. "Lots of killers show a nice face to the world. Besides, we can't do anything else right now. Going back to New West would probably bring the cops down on us. If we give it a day, maybe they'll think we've learned our lesson. If we are going to investigate Penelope Whitehall, we need some leverage against her. And we need to eliminate any other suspects."

Matthieu pointed to the screen. He'd been busy Googling while Val sulked, and I tried to pretend I was the adult in the situation. "Look, Val, we have a report on Madam Penelope," he said.

On the screen, there was a list of links. Matthieu had struck riches. Penelope was a bit of a publicity hound. "Did you find anything other than development business?"

"Yes. She doesn't seem to be shy when it comes to her profile." Matthieu pulled out his notebook and started scribbling. "Lu, what do you know about these organizations?" He slid the book to her.

She scanned the short list. "The first two are for business networking. I know some people who belong to them. I'll make a few coffee dates to see what I can get for you." She pointed to one of the items. "This one is a sorority group. I don't remember seeing her there."

Val gave up her sulk and moved to look over Lu's shoulder. "You are a sorority girl?"

Lu laughed. "What? You think there are only big boobed blonds in sororities? They let us Asians in too."

"I guess. I didn't really give it any thought. So, you are a sorority sister of the bitch?"

"I don't know. Matthieu, what does the article say about her involvement?"

Despite Lu's comments, Penelope was exactly what I imagined when I thought about sororities. She was cold, self-centered, and bitchy.

"Here it is. Ah, regardless of the title of this blog entry that Ms. Penelope has posted, she is not a member of your sorority, my dear. She was attending one of the fund-raising events that you organized. It seems she made a donation of two hundred dollars to the event which was to pay for legal representation for trafficked women."

"Two hundred bucks," Val snorted. "She probably paid more than that for lunch that week."

"It's not about what she should have given, Val," Lu said, sounding like she meant it.

As much as I knew charities needed small donations too, I

agreed with Val. "Okay so if someone wasn't looking too deeply, she looks like she belongs in a group that does charity work. She's building a background for some reason. Let's look deeper."

We spent an hour searching and reading articles about Penelope Whitehall. As far as I could see, she didn't have any real background. The only thing that was solid in her online presence was the real estate sales she'd made. She'd earned a pile of Salesperson of the Month awards.

"We need to eat," Lu said as we started to brainstorm more searches. "We'll go in circles without fuel."

I pushed away from the table and my iPad. Matthieu had sent us links to our devices so we could look up more information in a short time. "I'll help you."

"No, just sit there. Val and I made dinner." Lu placed a pile of cutlery on the table and then left the room.

"Did you notice them leave to prepare a meal?" I asked Matthieu as I distributed the knives and forks.

"Yes, but you were deeply into the educational research on Ms. Whitehall. Don't worry. It was not that long ago."

The two cooks carried in bowls of pasta and bread. "Put away the electronics," Lu ordered. "We can talk about what we've found, but we'll be unplugged for food."

Val poured a new bottle of wine and I stopped her from adding a glass for herself. "Hey, come on. If we were in France, I'd be able to drink." She looked at Matthieu.

He chuckled. "That is true, but we are not in France." He served the penne. "Perhaps you can have a small glass when we prove you are innocent."

"Fine." There wasn't much attitude left in her voice. I figured she was just trying it on.

I tasted the penne and realized how hungry I was. It was quiet for a few minutes while we all stuffed ourselves. Matthieu was the first to break the silence. "I have noticed one thing that might be useful. There are two patterns to the information we have found. The first we saw quickly. Anything that seems to make this woman seem caring, or human, doesn't hold up to scrutiny."

I nodded. "Yeah, it's all image and not that deep. I was hoping we would find something that we could use to get her off our backs. I'm not sure there's a way to get leverage on her."

"There has to be something." Val started to clear the table. "If she keeps complaining about us, we won't be able to investigate." I tried to argue that there would be other suspects, but I wasn't so sure anymore.

"Ah, I said there were two patterns." Matthieu grabbed another bottle of wine and opened it.

Lu gave him a playful punch. "Cut the mysterious act, my love."

I was trying to remember all the conversations over the information, but I had been too engrossed in my own research to pay attention to it all.

Matthieu shrugged. "I noticed that the older information is very light. It seems that she has become more interested in sharing details, whether they are real or not, in the last five years."

That was definitely something we could dig into.

Val sat beside me. "So, you think she's in witness protection? Or maybe she's a spy?"

I shook my head. "No, Val. I would be surprised if she was either. She wouldn't have involved the cops if she was. She would keep a low profile."

AN HOUR LATER, Val was heading upstairs for the night. "What time are we meeting tomorrow?"

I looked at Matthieu. He shook his head and said, "I must go to court to testify in the Watson case."

Lu shrugged. "I have to go to the dentist. Val, do you want to come?"

Rolling her eyes, Val made a face.

I bowed to the inevitable. Val would be with me while I investigated. "I'll pick you up around nine?" If we got to New West too early, we wouldn't find anyone to talk to. "I'll buy us breakfast and we'll maybe talk to Angelique again." We hadn't found out much about Angelique. She also didn't have much history online. The difference between her and Penelope was that Angelique hadn't changed her behavior lately.

"Fine." She sounded tired rather than teenage.

"Maybe we'll get a break." My phone buzzed. "Unknown number. Probably a telemarketer." I answered the call anyway.

"Ms. Deacon?" The woman asked before I could say my name. "It's Mrs. Irons. Do you remember me, dear?"

"Yes." I waved to Val to join us. "I remember you. How are you Mrs. Irons?"

"Oh, I'm as fine as I can be. You know it's always a good day when you wake up alive at my age." She gave a little laugh.

I pressed speaker. "You have a lot of mornings ahead of you, I'm sure."

"Well that may be true. I have some news for you and Val."

"She's right here."

"Hello, dear. I have a couple of new clients for you. That is if you want them."

Val reached for the phone, but I pulled away. "Yes, Mrs. Irons, I am taking on new clients. Can we see you tomorrow?"

"Well, I'm busy tomorrow. Come the next day. That will be perfect. I'll bake cookies."

I was all for Val increasing her business, but Mrs. Irons wouldn't call my number for that. "I'll bring her by, Mrs. Irons."

"Good. Now, dear, I called because I have some news for you about that club."

"The kink club?" Val asked.

"Yes, the sex club. I asked my friends, like I said I would."

I tried not to sound impatient, either she was trying to make the story better, or she was just a dithering type.

Before I prompted, she continued. "Well, they were concerned about me until I assured them I didn't want to join."

Val snickered. "Are you sure you don't?"

"Oh, young lady, I don't need to get kinky at my age. Simple sex is good enough for me. And don't you go telling my daughter that either."

I tried not to visualize, but I noticed that Matthieu and Lu were looking impressed.

"Well, they said I should talk to old Mr. Yareny. He is a member, apparently."

"Don't take that chance." I could follow up on the lead, if there was a link between the club and the murder. Mrs. Irons would be over her head. "I'll talk to him if you can give me the contact information."

"I already talked to him, Ms. Deacon. I'm not afraid of that silly old man. He didn't really want to tell me about the club. I didn't want the details of his sex life of course. When I convinced him of that, he was more than willing to tell me everything."

I waved at Matthieu to give me something to write on. He slid my notebook and pen across the table. "Go ahead, Mrs. Irons."

"Well, the club has been in operation for a couple of years. It's a small group of people, and it's run by a woman who is... Well, Mr. Yareny said she's used to getting her own way."

"Did you get her name?" Val asked.

I gave her a stern look and mouthed, "Let me ask the questions."

She rolled her eyes, but still stepped back from the phone.

Mrs. Irons continued, "I did ask. I don't know if he didn't know her name, or if he just didn't want to tell me."

That's why I needed to talk to him. Getting information was about more than just asking direct questions. "Will you introduce me to Mr. Yareny? I may be able to get him to talk to me."

"I can, but I worry that it may all be in his imagination. I'm afraid he's starting to drift into Alzheimer's or something like it. I do wish I had been able to get you something concrete."

"You did a great job. Don't get yourself any closer to this. Give me Mr. Yareny's information and I'll ask him myself."

"I don't know that he'll talk to you if I just send you to him. I'll invite him to tea and then we can all chat. That way he'll be more comfortable, and more likely to remember the details."

I knew a shut down when I heard one. "Okay, when would you like us to come?"

"You are coming the day after tomorrow anyway. I'll invite him for eleven am. Is that acceptable?"

"That's great. I'll be bringing a colleague who might make your friend more comfortable."

"A man, you mean."

"Yes, a man. It might be easier for Mr. Yareny to talk to another man."

There was silence. "Yes, that makes sense, dear. I hope you find proof that Val is innocent before then."

"We do too, Mrs. Irons."

"Well, I'll let you get back to your investigation. Goodnight. And good night to you, Val."

"You have very interesting sources of information, Charity," Matthieu said. "Old ladies and sex clubs?"

I laughed. "You get it where you find it, Matthieu. Will you be okay to meet us there?"

"Yes, I will talk to this Mr. Yareny."

Val slumped into a chair. "What if he's losing it? What if his information isn't good?"

"What if it is good? This mystery woman might be a lead. She might even be the killer. If she's used to getting her own way, maybe Mr. Schell did something she didn't like."

"Or maybe she's just a dominatrix." Val seemed determined to look on the dark side. "I'm going to bed."

When she was upstairs, I looked at Lu. "So, do you have any idea why she's suddenly Ms. Pessimism?"

"I don't know. Maybe the fact that she's facing prison for a murder she didn't commit. Or that she's in danger of losing the business she set up because she can't work on it and investigate." She shrugged. "Or maybe it's just because she's eighteen."

"Well, I can help her with two of those things." I grabbed my bag. "I'll see you when I pick her up."

NINE

I drove over to Lu's the next morning and passed her in the driveway. We stopped the cars to chat.

"Val is still asleep." Lu glanced at the door. "Do you have your key? Matthieu is already on his way to court."

I dug my keys out of my purse and held them up. "I always have my spares with me. See you tonight? Maybe we'll be able to get Val out of your hair. I know you don't much care for having her here." I wasn't blaming her. Having a teenager dumped on you can't be fun.

Lu smiled. "It's not that I don't like her. She's a real survivor. You should hear some of the ideas she has for new businesses. But yes, it will be nice to have our home back." She drove off and I pulled up in front of the door.

Inside, the house was quiet. For a go-getter, Val wasn't an early riser. I called out as I mounted the stairs, but there was no response. The door to her room was closed. I knocked and called again – nothing.

I pushed the door open. "Val, you have to get up. If we're going..." The bed was made, and there was no sign of Val.

My heart dropped. Had she packed up and left? She'd been

stroppy last night, but I thought it was just teenage hormones and pressure from the investigation. It couldn't be the same as the last time she'd disappeared. That was after we'd found her sister and broken the gang, and the case was over.

I pulled out my phone. Who could I call?

Not Jake, unless maybe she'd gone to New West early. If he'd seen her there, maybe he could keep her on set until I arrived. I pressed his number, but just got his voicemail. I hung up.

I called Val's phone and got voicemail. "Val, call me, please. We were supposed to meet at Lu's and clearly you're not here."

There was nothing for it but to head out and start the investigation myself. If she didn't turn up, I would have to make sure Lu got her bail money back. The only way to do that was to find the murderer, or at least proof that Val wasn't the murderer, before she had to go to court.

I locked up the house and pulled out of the drive. It was going to be an hour before I got to New Westminster. I had plenty of time to imagine what I would say to Val when I found her. And to formulate a plan on how to get dirt on Penelope to get her out of our way so we could concentrate on the murder.

I PULLED into the parkade and headed over to Jake's chair. The crew were busy setting up a shot, so we had time for a quick kiss.

"Where's your shadow?"

I glanced around to make sure no cops were nearby. "Disappeared. I'm hoping she's here somewhere. I need to get to her before the cops do."

"That kid, Rory, was looking for her. Maybe he can help."

I glanced toward the craft table and saw Rory refreshing a

platter of vegetables. "I don't know. If the cops find out she's missing, it could mean a bail violation."

Jake chuckled. "He won't tell anyone. Give him a chance. He likes her."

"That was obvious yesterday. Okay. Let me do some nosing around and I'll get him when he's on a break."

The director called Jake, so I waved goodbye.

I was tempted to go drop in on the development office, but I couldn't afford the attention. I decided to check out Penelope's competitors. Maybe there was some gossip I could work with to get a lead or make her mad enough to say the wrong thing.

"Ms. Deacon."

The voice broke into my little daydream about Penelope's reaction when we found out her secret. I turned around as I answered. It was the skinny cop. "Yes?"

"I hope you took our warning seriously. I don't want to have to take you in for harassment."

What the hell did this Penelope have on the cops that they made such a point of protecting her? "I heard what you said. I'm just hanging out."

"See that you do." He looked over my shoulder. "Where is Ms. Wei?"

Keep it light. "Why?"

He narrowed his eyes. "She's on bail."

"That means she needs to be with one of three people, not just in my custody."

"Is she with one of the others?"

I couldn't outright lie. "Does it matter? I mean, unless you find her out on her own, don't you just assume she's sticking to the bail requirements?"

He twisted his lips into a sneer. "Maybe we should check on her. Have her report in before end of day." He nodded at me and then turned away.

What the hell? Did he think this was his little empire? If I couldn't find Val before three, I'd have to call her lawyer to deal with it. I wasn't going to be able to juggle all of these problems and clear her name.

I decided to put off gossiping with realtors for scouring the town for Val. At least it wasn't a large city, there was some hope. Step one, find Val. Step two, clear her name.

I headed back to get Rory as a reinforcement. When I reached the craft table, he was just standing there looking bored.

"Hey, Charity." He glanced around. "Where's Val?"

It wasn't good for my ego to keep hearing that question. It's not like I just existed to accompany Val around. "I need to talk to you about that."

I filled him in, and he told his boss, who turned out to be his aunt, that he was taking off.

"I can go down where the homeless people are." He picked up his camera. "It would be a great piece for my doc. You think they would be happy to help if I told them Val was in trouble?"

He was eager at least. "Just be discreet. Remember the cops can't know she's in violation."

"Yeah, right. No cops."

We agreed to meet in an hour to check in. I headed over to Val's apartment. I didn't think it would be that easy, but it was a place to start.

I GOT to Val's and knocked on the door. I wasn't surprised when no one answered. I leaned against the door and listened but there was no noise. It felt wrong to just walk away, so I dialed Val's number. "I don't know why you are playing this game, Val," I said to her voicemail. "Call me so we can figure it out."

I felt like I was being pulled in different directions. My

priorities changing every time I thought I was in control. Having to find out where Val got to, meant I couldn't follow up the few leads we had. There were so few leads I was really scared that we wouldn't be able to clear Val's name.

If the police were really not considering other suspects, Val could be looking at a prison sentence. I knew she didn't think it would be that serious, but she should.

I sent her a text. If it was going to take nagging, I'd do it. If she ended up hating me, it would be worth it to get her cleared.

It was time to work on the next priority, finding another credible suspect. Since Rory was looking in the only other place I thought Val might be, I decided to go to Ink & Needles and talk to Angelique. If Rory didn't have anything to report when we met, I'd have to think about our next steps. At that point the whole priority would go to finding Val before we had to confess she wasn't with any of the adults who were supposed to watch her.

TEN

As I passed the shoot, I noticed they were packing up. I couldn't remember exactly where they would be shooting next, but it was somewhere in town and Jake would let me know tonight. It would be a mixed blessing if they left. It was great to see Jake every day, but it was also a pain to have to be quiet when we were on set. And, maybe, when Val showed up, we could check out that club.

I pushed open the door to Ink & Needles to see a biker standing at the counter. From what I could see, there wasn't much skin left for him to offer for art. He had full sleeves. A back tattoo peeked above his tee shirt and went into his hairline. His legs were covered in baggy jeans and chaps, so maybe he had room there. I waited as Angelique discussed his next project and cringed at what I thought I heard. He was going to get something branded. She glanced at me a couple of times, but there was no expression on her face. I wondered if she was trying to hide something, and then dismissed the suspicion. There didn't seem to be any motive for her to be the killer.

He nodded to me as he left, and I nodded back to be polite.

Angelique finished making notes in a sketch pad before motioning me over. "Hey, where's that handsome French guy?"

I laughed. "He's in court today. And then he's going to meet his fiancé for lunch." I hoped she was just kidding, but it didn't hurt to remind her that Matthieu wasn't available.

"So, did you decide on some ink?" She doodled something on a new page in the pad. "Something like this would be great for your street cred."

I looked at it. She'd drawn a spider sitting in the middle of a web. The spider had blue eyes like mine. "Uh, thanks, but I like my street cred just the way it is."

She laughed. "Maybe another time. What can I do for you?"

"I was hoping you had some more information about Mr. Schell. Or anything that might help clear Val's name." I hated that pathetic sound in my voice. It was there because we weren't making any progress. I needed to buck up.

She winked. "You know that the man was involved in a bit of the dark side, right."

"Yeah, I heard. Do you know who owns that sex club?"

"Just because I do tattoos, doesn't mean I'm into kink." The long fingernail that she tapped on the counter wasn't helping her attempt at innocence.

"I didn't say you were."

She roared out a laugh. "Good point. Okay, I guess I'm a bit sensitive. I've had a few people in here trying to make me out as some kind of bad influence on the area. Like I'm bringing the tone of the street down. Fat chance with that lap dancing place still operating."

Interesting. "People, or just one?"

She shrugged. "Mostly just one. That developer, Penelope the ice witch. And I suspect she was behind the others."

Penelope hadn't managed to make any friends. "She does like to get her way. I've felt her disapproval too."

Angelique put the sketch pad away. "Val thinks the Ice Queen killed Mr. Schell. Do you have any proof?"

I would have to tell Val to be careful who she shared her theories with. "No, other than maybe it has something to do with the sex club."

She shrugged. "I wish I could help. I haven't found any of the papers I said I'd look through. Sorry, I've been busy. I'll get to it this afternoon, promise. Maybe Matthieu can come by to pick up anything I find?"

"Maybe." I would make sure he didn't come alone. "Give me a call if you find anything. I'm around town all day."

"I will. I like Val, and I don't think she'd do anything like that." She flipped open an appointment book. "I don't have anything booked after eleven. I'll start digging through boxes then."

I thanked her and headed for the street. Just as I reached for the handle, the door opened toward me. I stepped back to avoid getting hit as it swung hard and a uniformed cop strode in. "Ms. Roman?" He asked as he walked toward the counter. I couldn't tell if he didn't know I was there, or if he didn't care that I was.

I decided to stay, just in case Angelique needed someone to... I don't know, close the shop when they dragged her away.

She didn't seem worried. "That's me, officer."

He held out a photo. "Do you know this man?"

Angelique took the photo and looked at it closely. "Yeah, it's the guy who works in that developer's office. I did some ink on him last week."

I moved closer to the counter. She handed me the photo before the cop could take it back.

It was Ken.

He lay face down on a pile of rubble, dead. It was clearly him, I wondered briefly why Angelique had to look so closely. "What happened?"

The cop reached for the photo. "You knew him?"

I nodded. "Just met him in the office. What happened?" Maybe if I kept asking, he'd tell us.

He turned back to Angelique. "How well did you know him?"

"We talked a couple of times to get the design right. Then it took about an hour to do the ink. Other than that, I didn't know him at all."

He took out a notebook. "Do you mind telling me where you were last night between eleven thirty and two am?"

"That's pretty specific," I said before Angelique could answer. This was the only opportunity I might have to ask questions. I figured as soon as he had his answers, the cop would be on his way to the next interrogation. And I didn't like the way he was pushing Angelique; did he think she was a suspect?

He turned and looked me over. "Your name?"

I had to admit that he was good. I gave him my name and my business card.

He asked me for my alibi. Maybe he thought he'd catch the killer and get a promotion.

"I was at home. My boyfriend can verify it."

He made a note and then went back to Angelique. He didn't ask again, just stood waiting for her answer.

"I was at home as well. I don't have anyone to verify it."

He made notes and then put his book away. "We'll be in touch if we need anything more."

We watched him leave.

"That was weird," Angelique said.

"Yes. I wouldn't be surprised if we both had to answer more questions. They wouldn't be canvassing the area if he died of natural causes." And maybe it was the same person who killed Mr. Schell. That wasn't going to be good for Val. I had no idea when she took off last night.

I headed back to meet Rory, wondering about the implications of another body turning up while Val was alone. If she didn't have an alibi, she might have to spend some time in jail. Not that I wouldn't fight it, but even I could tell that she was looking like a good suspect.

The actors, cameras, and every other piece of evidence of Hollywood North had packed up and gone. The street looked normal. I could see Rory leaning against a bridal shop, but no Val. I pulled out my phone to see if she'd contacted me, but there was no message.

"Hey, Charity." Rory peeled away from the shop and waved.

"How did it go?" Maybe he had a lead, or something that would help.

"Huh?" He looked around and then reached into the doorway beside him, pulling Val onto the street. "Yeah, I guess it went well." A grin lit up his face.

I joined them as anger replaced my fear for her. "Where have you been? You are supposed to stay with us."

"Yeah I know. I was worried about the people on the street. They rely on me to bring them food. I kinda thought I would be back before you noticed, but I couldn't get a cab."

"And your phone died?" It was hard to stay mad when she was worried about people like that, but I was willing to give it a try.

"That's right. Look, don't have a bird. I stayed out of the cops' way and I didn't get dragged off to jail. Lu's bond is still safe." She dug into the pocket of her jacket. "I found something."

I couldn't just let that go. "Next time you want to help your friends, ask me to come along."

She looked up from the object in her hand. "Sure. Look. I found this."

She was holding out a woman's glove. Beige leather, although it looked expensive, so it was probably called sandstone blush or something. There was some kind of stain on the fingertips. "Where did you find that?"

She grinned. "I dug around in the alleys and stuff around Mr. Schell's store. I thought maybe the killer tossed something away, and I was right."

I hated to deflate her excitement, but a killer wouldn't be stupid enough to toss one glove close to the body. And she was holding the glove in her bare fingers, and it had been in her pocket. It was worse than useless. It could be used against her. "It's got your fingerprints on it, Val."

"I told her that," Rory said and turned to her. "You should have used a baggie like it was dog poop. Don't you watch TV?"

She glared at him. "No, I don't, and I was trying to clear my name."

Rory didn't take the hint and stop talking, "You think the cops missed something like that when they searched?"

"It was in an alley, under a cardboard box," she huffed.

I held up my hand for peace. "Don't cause a scene. The last thing we need is for someone to call the cops." I looked around the street. It was getting busy. "There's been another murder. Let's get off the street. Come on." I led them to the Waves Coffee House, and we sat at a table in the back corner with our lattes.

When we were settled, I started talking. "We'll get the glove to your lawyer. He can figure out the best way to deal with it. Do you think there's someone who can vouch for you last night?"

"Why? Do the cops know I wasn't with Lu?" She was trying to sound brave, but I heard the little quaver in her voice.

"No, but that's because they haven't checked. If none of your friends on the street come forward, you don't have an alibi for a second murder." I felt mean being so blunt, but I didn't know how else to tell her.

"Whoa, really?" Rory had a glint of interest in his eye that made me think he'd be good at show business. He had an instinct for news. He pulled a tablet out of his backpack and started making notes.

"Charity, I was with the street people, and then I went home to sleep. I can, maybe, get someone to vouch for me until one am. When did it happen?"

"I need to get the details, but it was within that timeframe. Is there any way we can talk to your friends now?"

She shook her head. "They get moved along during the day. I think most of them hit an early Skytrain and get downtown so they can get good spots for panhandling. Um, who was killed?"

I filled her in on the little information I had. Rory stopped writing to ask us who Ken was, and why the cops might think Val killed him.

"I didn't do it, Rory."

"Yeah, yeah, babe. I know you didn't. I said why would the cops think you did?"

It was a great question. "You know, maybe we'll have better luck answering that question instead of trying to find the killer," I said.

Val jerked forward and whispered, "We need to find the killer."

I nodded. "Yes, but first we need you off the suspect list." I had a bad feeling that there was still only one name on that list. "Then we can easily investigate the case, or cases, I guess."

I explained to Rory about Penelope and why she might want to cause problems.

He made some more notes. "Do you think she might have killed Ken to make the cops lock you up?"

"Dude, that is crazy." Val slapped Rory's arm. "No one would do that."

I agreed. Even the ice queen wouldn't kill someone just to get rid of us. "Look, let's go check you in at the station so the cops don't come looking for you. I can try to get some information from them, and then if I do, we can follow up on it."

"Can I come with you?" Rory put the tablet away. "I can use this stuff in my documentary."

I raised an eyebrow at Val.

She shrugged. "Sure, why not. Just don't call me babe again."

He grinned. "Yes, Val."

I gathered up the cups and placed them on the counter before we went out to the street. "Let me do the talking, okay?"

"I'll behave as long as they don't push me." Val started marching toward the station.

"Yeah," Rory agreed. "Will you ask some questions for me?"

I ignored the feeling in my gut that I was going to regret Rory's presence. "Two questions, and you better have them ready before we go in."

"Okay. Ask them if they have a suspect for this murder and ask them if they think the two are related." He nodded as though he'd picked the two best questions off a list.

They weren't bad questions, but I was planning to get that information anyway. I'm sure he would get better at it with practice.

ELEVEN

There was a crowd in the police station when we entered, people filled the chairs. A couple of bearded, leather clad men lounged against the wall. I marched up to the counter trying to give the impression I was important enough to pay attention to.

Val and Rory kept close behind me.

"I need to talk to Detective Reynolds."

The woman looked at me, then back to her papers. "I'll let him know, just wait over there somewhere." She was obviously not impressed with my attitude.

'Over there' was next to the two men. We stood together rather than sitting and watched three more people come in before Detective Reynolds stepped through the door behind the receptionist. I moved toward him.

"Joseph Wilkins?" Detective Reynolds called.

I kept moving toward him but was cut off by the blond bearded guy. The two disappeared into the back before I could say anything.

"Don't worry, lady. He's just checking in. You'll be back there in five minutes." The red bearded guy looked me over. It made me feel a little dirty.

Val leaned out from behind Rory. "I didn't realize people had to check in with the cops."

"Detective Reynolds likes to make sure people stay out of trouble. I think he's trying to be a good guy, but he comes across like an asshole." He looked at me again. "What did you do to get his attention?"

I gave Val a glare to keep her from answering. "I didn't do anything. I'm just here to ask him some questions."

"About what?"

This guy was getting too nosy for me. "Just something we're looking into. I'm a private investigator."

He looked impressed. "Huh. So, you investigating that guy's death?"

Rory shifted and I expected to see a camera come out of his backpack. I blocked him and asked, "Which guy?"

"Good point. I guess the last guy."

I shrugged. "My client is interested in Mr. Schell's death. Did you know him?"

"Can't say I did." He pushed away from the wall. "It looks like it's your turn."

I followed his head point and saw Detective Reynolds staring at me. The blond bearded man strode toward us.

I turned to Val and Rory. "Stay here."

"No," Val said before striding past me.

I hurried to get in front of her, worried at how Detective Reynolds would react to her pushiness.

"Ms. Deacon. Thanks for coming in." He held out his hand to shake.

I stopped and looked at his hand. I shook it and waited for whatever was coming. What was he trying to do with this mister nice guy act?

"Come on back to my office." He turned without checking

to see if we were following. So, he was back to playing the hard-nosed asshole?

We followed him past an open room where two detectives occupied cubicles, into a small office that was more like a high walled cubicle. One wall had a window that looked out over the alley into the brick wall of another building. The desk and chair were placed so the occupant was looking into the open space, not at the view. Two folding chairs faced the desk. I sat and Val took the other chair. Rory stood behind Val, taking his phone out and turning it on.

"Put the phone away, young man." Detective Reynolds shoved a file folder to the side.

"Why?"

Reynolds glared at Rory.

"Okay, it's away." He slid the phone into his pocket.

I didn't want to waste time. "You can see Val is with me. Are we good on the bail conditions?"

"Yes."

Formalities over, I dug for information. "I heard about the new murder."

"Yes."

"When did it happen?"

"That information isn't public yet."

"How can we prove Val had nothing to do with it?" I wanted information, but I would settle for clearing Val.

"I haven't asked you to do that." He flipped the file open. I could see reports, but not read them. "The time of death is approximately one am."

Val sighed. "I was sleeping."

Detective Reynolds nodded. "I imagine most people are at that time. Anything else?" He gave me a glance as he leaned his elbows on the desk.

It was clear there was something he wasn't telling us. And

he wanted me to know he was holding back. I couldn't think why he was playing this game, but we needed to get back to finding out who killed Mr. Schell. "Do we need to call Val's lawyer?"

Detective Reynolds glanced over my shoulder. "No. We have information leading to another suspect. I need you to keep this confidential." He waited until we agreed. "The information gives us another suspect in the Schell murder as well."

That could be good news for Val, if the cops were willing to be reasonable. "I'll be passing that along to Val's lawyer."

"That's fine, but no further. We don't want to jeopardize the investigation." He flicked a glance over my shoulder again. It hit me that he was checking for his boss. "I think you can let us take it from here."

Val jerked forward. "No, we'll keep looking."

I patted her knee. "I won't get in your way."

He closed the file as if shutting me out from the case. "Has your investigation led anywhere so far?" he asked.

The only lead we had was about the sex club and we needed to get more information before I would call it a real lead. "No. A few rumors, but nothing that I have any confidence in. Anything on your end?"

"Nice try. You know I can't share anything with you. Don't interfere with my investigation, and we'll be fine. If you find anything that might lead to the killer, you call me."

Since I couldn't arrest anyone by myself, that didn't need to be said. "Of course. What about the complaints from Ms. Whitehall? Can we talk to her?"

He scowled. "Why would you need to talk to her?"

That was a bit defensive. "The latest victim was her assistant."

"I thought you were investigating the Schell case. Why would you care about Ken Leeman's?"

I stood and motioned Val and Rory to head out. "It's too much of a coincidence that the two murders happened so close to each other. I'm sure you're looking at them as the same killer. Otherwise, you wouldn't be letting Val off the hook."

He nodded. "Just stay out of our way."

TWELVE

There wasn't much to do for the rest of the day, so we decided to head back to Vancouver. I called Lu, and Val's lawyer, with the news.

"Can we pick up my stuff from Lu's?" Val asked as we headed back to the car. "It's not like I need to stay with her anymore. I'm off the hook, right?"

I didn't like the idea of her being alone when there was a murderer running around. "You aren't off the hook. The cops still think you're a suspect, regardless of what he said. Do you really want to stay in your apartment rather than at Lu's?" I couldn't trust her to stay safe and not start asking questions that could get her killed

"Her place is nice. It's just too far away when I don't have a car." She brightened. "I could borrow a car. That might work."

Rory bumped her gently. "I could pick you up. Where is her place?"

"On the North Shore. I was kidding about staying there. I need to be home." She glanced over her shoulder. "Where's your car?"

He reddened. "I didn't bring it today. I'm on transit. I guess I should go. When will we meet up tomorrow?"

I waited for Val to give me a hint whether she wanted Rory to join us, but she just shrugged.

"We'll call you when we've figured it out." We were meeting Mrs. Irons and her friend tomorrow. Having a camera there might put a stop to any candid information.

I hated the look of disappointment that descended over him. "Yeah, cool. You have my number. Uh, bye, Val."

She must have felt sorry for him because she gave him a quick hug. "Thanks for being there today. We'll call you. I promise."

He nodded and left us at the car.

I unlocked it and got in. "It's going to be a bear to get over to Lu's right now. Why don't you come over to my place? We'll have dinner and then go to Lu's later."

She slid into the passenger seat. "Okay, but I want to sleep at my place."

"Okay." I could sympathize with the feeling, but I didn't want her alone tonight.

"Good. How about pizza? I like Lu and all, but she never lets me eat real food."

I knew what she meant. Sometimes a girl just needs take-out. I called Jake before starting the car. He was at home, and willing to get the pizza on the table by the time we got there.

Val fiddled with the radio. "Maybe Jake could help us. I bet he could get information out of people if he wanted."

I tried to picture Jake as an investigator. He was not happy that I made my living that way. Working together might just break our relationship. "No, we can deal with this."

She was silent until we parked the car. "I kinda missed staying in your living room. It was, I don't know, cozy."

I took advantage of the opportunity. "You left pretty fast."

"I know. Emma was afraid that they would come after her. I had to make sure she was safe. Sorry."

It was good to hear the words, but I realized that her abandonment of me didn't hurt so much now. "I'm glad you found a new life. Do you hear from Emma?"

Val looked out the window. "She calls once in a while. I think she wants to put that stuff behind her."

I hadn't had a lot of contact with Emma, but I didn't like her much. Sure, she'd probably saved Val's life by getting her away from her parents' murder. All I knew about her was that she'd led Val into prostitution. Then, after Val and I rescued her from some pretty vicious gang members, she'd taken her away. You would think she'd stick around after all that, but it turned out she'd abandoned Val pretty quickly.

The pizza delivery guy was at the security gate when we arrived. I paid and flipped the lid a crack; pepperoni and pineapple. "Why don't you stay overnight? We can get your stuff in the morning."

She held her hand out for the pizza box so I could unlock the door. "That sounds good. I guess there's no rush to find the killer now I don't have to prove it's not me."

"We won't stop investigating, Val. I know Mr. Schell was important to you." As I unlocked the door, I saw Jake leaving his house a few doors away from mine.

"I've got the wine." He held up a bottle. "I think a little celebration of Val's freedom is in order."

I WAS WASHING dishes after dinner while Val and Jake pulled out some DVDs for a movie night. I looked at the pile of cases on the floor. "Only one movie. We need to get up early and get you sorted out, Val."

Jake joined me in the tiny kitchen. "Why don't you let it go now? Val is safe and you can go back to your usual cases. The cops can deal with the murders." He said it so gently it was almost easy to just agree. The problem was my gut tightened at the thought of going back on my promise to Val. "Val worked for the first victim. She liked him, and she's not going to just let it go."

He gave me a hug. "It's not your problem."

"Hey what's going on in there?" Val shouted.

I glared at Jake. "Just making some tea. You want some?"

"I'm fine. I think I've had enough to drink," she said.

I threw a tea towel at Jake and hissed, "Don't bring this up again. She'll just get into trouble trying to find the killer without me."

"She's not your kid." He was getting that stubborn look on his face. The one that used to make me feel like he was trying to control me. Now it just made me mad.

I told myself not to yell. "I know. But she's a kid. I don't want to read about her death in the paper."

He threw up his hands in surrender. "Fine, I'll let it go. But keep Matthieu close, and let the cops do the dangerous stuff."

I plugged in the kettle. "I promise."

Val looked up from the DVD player as I came back to the living room. "Have you finished arguing about me?"

I hoped she was guessing. "Were you listening?"

"It was hard not to hear," she admitted. "This place isn't exactly large."

I'd forgotten that. It was big enough for me but add another person and my home got small fast. I just didn't add anyone else very often. "Sorry. Jake likes you. He just wants to keep me safe."

"He's right. It is dangerous, and you don't owe anything." She looked away from me.

I sat on the floor beside her. "Are you willing to give up and let the cops take over?"

"No."

"Okay then we're still on the case. Start the movie." I got up and dug a blanket out of the linen cupboard. "You can sleep on the couch tonight."

THIRTEEN

The next morning, Rory was waiting for us at the entrance to the parking lot. Val saw him first.

She twisted to look at him as we drove past. "Why is he hanging around?"

I glanced at her as I waited while the car in front to maneuvered into a space. "Are you serious? He likes you."

She clicked her tongue, a slight improvement on rolling her eyes. "I figured that out. I don't get why he doesn't take the hint that I don't like him."

"I didn't see you giving him hints yesterday. I saw you giving signals." I parked but didn't get out of the car. "Val, if you want him to go away, you need to be clear."

She sighed. "I don't want to be rude. I guess I can put up with him for a while."

For someone who used to be in the sex trade, she didn't have a clue how to deal with men. "You guess, or you actually like him?"

"I don't know. What should I do?" She sounded so lost I couldn't tease her.

"Be nice to him, but don't give him any encouragement.

Maybe he'll lose interest." Hopefully it wouldn't coincide with her getting more interested.

She opened her door. "Okay. Maybe he'll be helpful, anyway."

We met him at the sixth street on-ramp. Today he was wearing baggy black-denim shorts, a flannel shirt, and Converse runners. "Hi, Val, so, what's on the agenda today?"

Val stared at him. "How are you going to do a documentary about homeless people without a camera?"

He patted the backpack hanging from his shoulder. "Don't worry babe, it's in here."

"Don't call me babe, it's condescending." She started up the short hill to Columbia. "I think we should go see Mrs. Irons."

I got between the two of them. "She invited us for eleven am. We have an hour to fill." I'd been thinking about where to start, and I wanted to see where they had found Ken's body. The news story we'd found on-line had a picture of the construction hording around Penelope's development. "We need to look around the building site. Rory, you can film there, but when we go to Mrs. Irons, keep the camera in the backpack. Okay?"

He nodded. "How are we going to get on the site?"

I pointed up the street. "We need to check it out. I'm hoping we can slip in down the side. There didn't seem to be any workers there the other day."

We headed toward the hording. It was set up with holes cut so people could see the progress. There wasn't any right now, and it looked like there hadn't been any for a while. There was police tape around a pile of rubble, other than that, it was a vacant lot.

"We could pull this board aside and sneak in," Val said.

Rory leaned against the board as if to test it. "There's no way we can do that without being seen, b... I mean, Val."

She glared at him. "Do you have a better idea?"

I had to agree with Rory. "I think we can get there from the back." I nodded toward a chain link fence that dipped as it attached to the wall. "It's low enough there for us to jump it."

We walked down to the fence. The dip didn't look as low from this close.

Val climbed up and dropped down to the other side. "Hang on." She pulled a couple of empty crates to the fence. Holding one up, she said, "Here, use this for a step." Rory grabbed the crate and placed it on the outside of the fence for me to use.

I kept lookout, but I'd been right about the fact no one was going to pay attention. It was odd, too, that there was no security on the site.

Rory tapped my arm. "You next."

I scrambled over and reached for his backpack. It had only taken minutes to get into the site, and now the only way people on Columbia Street would see us is if they looked through the hording windows. I was counting on the fact that people weren't interested in an empty hole. "Let's be quick."

Rory pulled out his camera and proceeded to document, and narrate, our activities. I tuned him out and started walking around the crime scene. Val stuck close to my heels.

"It doesn't look like there's anything here," she said. "I guess the cops did a good job in clearing out any clues."

"Be careful where you step." I pointed to a shoe print that had baked in a dried puddle. "Someone was wearing heels on a construction site."

"Probably Penelope. She's the developer here." Val said, bending to pick something up.

I grabbed her elbow. "Don't touch anything that might be a clue."

She straightened. "Yeah, I guess my fingerprints on evidence would be a bad idea. Look, there's a business card."

I bent and saw the edge of a card. The rubble on top was stained brown where the rain hadn't washed it clean of blood. I pulled a tissue out of my purse and used it to protect my fingers as I yanked the card free. It was Penelope Whitehall's. I wasn't surprised.

"I don't think this is any use as a clue. She could have dropped this any time, and it might have blown into the crime scene from anywhere on the lot." I tucked it into an envelope anyway.

"Hey guys," Rory called. "I think it's time to leave."

I looked where he pointed and saw faces in the hording windows. They were definitely watching us. No one seemed to be concerned yet, but Rory had a point, we needed to be gone before someone realized we didn't belong. "Be cool as we go. Maybe they won't notice we're leaving unconventionally." Not much chance, but confidence carried a lot of weight in most situations.

When we were over the fence, I made Rory toss the crate back. There was no need to leave an easy entrance for kids. We wandered away from the site as though there was nothing odd about us being there.

The visit to the construction site hadn't been a complete loss. It filled the time before we could head to Mrs. Irons' for tea and information. I wasn't convinced that the clues we found were going to help, but that didn't mean I was right. The blood on Penelope's card didn't mean she dropped it there, but it did mean that someone had dropped it before Ken's death, if it was his blood that is.

Before I rang the buzzer for Mrs. Irons' apartment, I looked Rory over. "Can you tuck in your shirt, or something, to keep your pants up?"

Val frowned. "I don't think Mrs. Irons will mind his look. It's not like he's the only guy in baggy shorts."

I watched while Rory tried to make himself more presentable. Tucking the shirt didn't help. He just looked nerdy and baggy. He must have noticed my disappointment because he grabbed his backpack and dug around. "Hang on. I think I can fix it." Pulling out a blue and red striped tie, he threaded it through his belt loops and tied it tight, so his shorts stayed at his waist. Then he pulled his shirt out to cover the mess. "See, I'm presentable." He looked down. "Well, more or less. I wasn't expecting to be corporate today."

I tried to imagine Rory in a suit and the image wouldn't stick. Although he had the tie for some reason, so maybe I was wrong. "Val, I don't know if this Mr. Yareny is conservative. The first rule of getting information is to avoid annoying your subject, unless you want to."

Rory grinned at Val. "Thanks for defending me, babe."

She turned and pushed the intercom button. "I wasn't."

MRS. IRONS BUSTLED into the kitchen to bring the coffee pot as we sat. "Oh, don't worry, dear. It's always nice to have young people visiting." She poured coffee. "Mr. Yareny will be here in a few minutes. He called just as you were coming up the elevator. Have a biscuit, Val."

Val nudged Rory as she reached for a shortbread cookie. He dug his phone out and turned down the ringer before putting it in his shirt pocket and taking his own cookie.

"How is your investigation going?" Mrs. Irons asked as she stirred cream into her cup.

"Slowly, but at least the police have another suspect now."

"That is good. I'm sure you'll make progress, dear." She jumped up to answer a knock on the door. Her eagerness made me wondered if she was sweet on Mr. Yareny.

He joined us in the dining area. He was probably about

Mrs. Irons' age, but where she was wiry and vital, he was squat and, from the few stubbly patches on his face, it looked like shaving on a regular basis was too much effort.

"You wanted information about the club." His voice was rusty as though he didn't use it much. "I won't give you any names. We keep our privacy." He dipped a cookie in his coffee.

I took out my notebook but put it beside me. "I can respect that. I'm looking for information about the owner. Do you know who that is?"

"Yep, but I ain't telling her name neither." He glared at me. "You know Schell was part of the club. You think it might have something to do with his death?"

I nodded.

"Well, no one at the club had reason to want him dead. He was a good neighbor, and an honest businessman. He kept his word, and that's rare."

This wasn't going to get us any closer to a suspect. I tried a new approach. "Was Ken Leeman a member of the club?"

"That's the feller that got killed? Found on the site of that new development? No, he wasn't. We tend toward the experienced type." He rubbed his short gray hair.

I tried to stifle the image of old people in bondage, because it creeped me out. "We're looking for something to help us find the person who killed Mr. Schell and Ken. Do you have any ideas that might help us?"

Before he could answer, Mrs. Irons refilled his coffee. "Ivan, don't be so obstructive. I think you can trust these young people with a few secrets. Charity is a private detective. She's used to keeping confidences. Isn't that right?"

I smiled, hoping it was reassuring, and said, "It is."

"Well, I know Val, but who's this shady looking character?" He pointed at Rory. "How does he fit in?"

Rory shifted in his seat. "I'm with Val." He was smart enough not to mention the documentary filmmaker part.

Val leaned toward Mr. Yareny. "He can be trusted. They're trying to help me. The police think I might have killed Mr. Schell."

Mr. Yareny huffed. "How do I know they aren't right?"

Val's face went white. I don't think she took the police's accusation seriously, but this was different. Before she could answer him, Mrs. Irons slapped his arm. "Now you stop being so mean, Ivan. I swear you are just saying things to get a reaction. Do you have any information that might help, or are you just going to eat my biscuits, and upset everyone?"

"I might. My granddaughter works for the police."

I perked up. "They were given a new suspect. Do you know who that is?"

He grunted. "I don't want to get my granddaughter in trouble."

Val patted his arm. "We won't tell where we got the information."

He looked at her hand and then at Rory. "Is she your girlfriend?"

Rory swallowed the cookie he was eating. "No, but I don't think you're her type either."

Mr. Yareny roared a laugh. "Okay, good point. My granddaughter tells me bits of information now and then. She tells me that the police are looking for a hobo calls himself, Broomie. Someone seen him around Schell's place, and near where they found that Ken guy." He looked away as he spoke and dipped another cookie in his cup.

I saw Val open her mouth to speak so I shook my head just once and rose. "Thanks, I think we have enough to go on. Mrs. Irons, you have been a lot of help."

We said our goodbyes and left them to their tea and cookies.

In the elevator, Val couldn't hold it in any longer. "Brummie, his name is Brummie. He wouldn't do this. He's gentle, and kind, and just down on his luck."

I held up a hand to hush her. "I don't know if Mr. Yareny was telling the truth about what he heard. Or if he was lying about not knowing anything we could use. But I know he was lying, and not good at it." People who lied well, didn't look away as they talked.

Rory pulled out his phone. "Would it help to hear it again? I recorded the whole thing."

I started to tell him that was illegal and we couldn't use the recording, but I stopped myself. "It might. Just remember if this leads to finding the killer, we never recorded anything. It would destroy any case the cops build."

FOURTEEN

There was no private place to listen to the recording except my car. We climbed in and Rory put it on speaker. We listened to Mr. Yareny dodge giving us information while he kept us talking.

"You think he actually knows something?" Rory asked from the back seat.

"I thought so at the time." I still did. "I also think he was trying to impress Mrs. Irons."

Val took the phone and hit replay. "Listen. I think he likes the person running the club. And I think it's that Whitehall chick."

"What makes you think that?" I didn't want Val to get fixated on one suspect. Although I would love it to be Penelope, and not just because she'd annoyed me with that complaint.

"I think she's the one who gave the cops Brummie's name."

"Val, babe... sorry." Rory laughed as Val threatened to punch him. "I'm just saying you can't blame her for everything just because you don't like her."

She glared at him. "I have a reason. She hated Brummie. I

saw her threaten him with a hammer. He was just sleeping on the site and she caught him."

Penelope was looking like a better suspect every time I learned more about her. But just because she hated a friend of Val's didn't mean she killed anyone. "That doesn't mean she owns the club. Or that she killed two people."

Val passed the phone Rory. "Fine. What's next? Do we go check out that club and see if we can find some clues?"

"We'll do that later tonight. When there won't be so many people around." The last thing we needed was to be caught trying to get into a sex club.

The car was getting stuffy, and it was affecting the mood. I had one idea where we could ask questions. "Let's get back to the construction site. I think there'll be workers on it now. Maybe they have some information."

We headed back to the site where Ken's body had been found. A block away from our destination, I dodged into an antique store, pulling Val with me. Rory followed without a pause.

The store had a musty smell that seemed to be a combination of furniture oil and mildewed fabric. The bay window had a table of knickknacks in front of it, but I could still lean over to see what was going on in the street.

Val yanked her arm out of my grasp. "What happened?"

I peeked through the window. "I saw Penelope turn into the construction site. She was carrying her hard hat and vest. I don't think it's a good idea for us to be there."

"No kidding." Val joined me at the window. "I guess we have to wait?"

Rory handed his backpack to Val. "No, b.... Uh. I have an idea." He pulled out his phone. "She doesn't know me. I could go looking for a job and ask some questions."

"Dude, that's a great idea." Val grabbed his backpack from

him and slung it over her shoulder, knees sinking with the weight as it settled. "Be careful, though. She's a killer."

"Val, we don't know that." I looked at Rory. He still had the tie holding his pants up, but he looked old enough to work on a building site. "She's right. It could be dangerous. If you feel threatened, get out and come tell us what you learned."

He grinned. "I won't have to report. Give me your phone."

I put my phone into his hand.

"Okay, this is how it will go." He traced the pattern to unlock my phone. Shocked, I asked him how he knew it. "You should get something more complicated and stop holding your phone up for anyone to see when you unlock." Ignoring my attempt to defend my lack of phone security, he flipped through the few apps I'd installed.

He finally glanced up. "I'll install an app to record the call. Then I'll call you when I get close. You answer and put yourself on mute. Then you can listen, and we'll have it recorded."

"Okay." I would have to tell Matthieu about this. It could come in handy when we were working a case together. "We'll have to wait somewhere else."

A middle-aged woman approached. "Are you looking for something in particular?"

I put on my professional smile and shook my head. "We were just browsing. You have some great stuff here."

She looked pleased. "We can search for any particular items, if you have something in mind."

Val stepped in, handing the woman her business card. "I might have someone who is looking for a few items. I'll drop by if I get any details. Let's go, guys."

I followed her out, Rory trailing behind.

Val grabbed Rory's sleeve. She gave him a hug. "You be careful. I might want to see you again."

He grinned and gave her a peck on the cheek before slouching toward the fencing around the building site.

Val rolled her eyes. "Don't get excited. He's not as bad as I thought." She watched him until my phone rang.

I answered it and pressed the mute button. "Not as bad as you thought? That's a beginning."

"Yeah. Look, when we're done, we have to go back to that store. I saw something."

I started to ask what, but the conversation started on Rory's end.

"Hey. How's it going?"

"What do you want, kid?"

"I was hoping to get some work. Anything going?"

"No, we've got all the guys we need."

"Can I leave you my phone number?"

"Sure."

Rory gave his number. "Hey, I heard some guy was found dead here."

"Yeah. Assistant to the boss."

"You know anything about it?"

"No. You a reporter?" The voice switched from interested to suspicious. "Maybe I should get the boss here. She doesn't like people nosing around."

"No, don't freak. I was just asking. Is that your boss? She's hot."

There was a long pause. "Yeah, you know what they say, beauty is skin deep. She's a bad woman to cross. And too many people have been asking about the body. It's slowing us down, and that doesn't make her happy."

"You might need me then. Hey, I gotta go. Maybe I can get some hours at another site. I want to take my girlfriend out to a nice place."

Val snorted at that.

A few minutes later, Penelope's voice cut through the conversation. Rory said 'bye' and left.

I took the call off mute when Rory said he was away from them and told him we'd be at the antique shop. "So, what did you see at the store?"

Val gave a quick grin. "Remember the glove I found? There's a pair almost like them in the store."

Rory was already inside when we stepped through the doorway.

"Here they are," he said, turning to the shopkeeper. "I told you they were on their way."

The woman looked relieved, making me wonder how sheltered she was that Rory scared her. He might be scruffy, but he wasn't threatening.

Val stepped forward and put her hand on his arm, implying that he was a potential good guy with the movement. "I noticed the gloves and had to come back and ask."

The woman reached under the glass counter between them and gently lifted out a pair of beige gloves with beadwork on the back of the fingers. "These? Yes, aren't they lovely. The beads are jet and they are hand sewn. The gloves were well taken care of. They are sixty years old, and they look almost new."

They just looked old fashioned to me.

Val wiped her hands before gently touching the beadwork. "Lovely. Are these the only pair?"

"No. I sold another pair last week to a businesswoman. Do you know Ms. Whitehall?"

Val nodded, with no indication of her hatred for Penelope.

I looked over Val's shoulder and said, "I know someone who would love this pair. Are they expensive?"

"Not for the workmanship." The woman flipped the small tag over and I saw $500 written neatly in violet pen.

"Thanks, I'll think about it."

FIFTEEN

Standing outside the store in the dim light that came through the narrow gap between the parking structure and the buildings, I tried to think about how to tie Penelope to the glove, and then the glove to the killings.

Val looked toward the construction site. "We are totally going to get her."

"Don't get excited. We have to be careful with this information. We don't want her to push back. She seems to be powerful. We have to find a way to cut off whatever she thinks is keeping her safe." I heard the rumble of a train approaching. It was about to get hard to hear. "Let's get lunch and figure this out."

Rory put his arm around Val, removing it rapidly when she glared at him. I had to admire his persistence. I figured it would take all he had to break through the shell Val had built around herself. When we got to the top of the hill, Rory looked around. "Too bad the filming has moved on. We could have eaten from the craft table."

I didn't feel like mooching food again, and there were more than a few choices. "How about Greek? I hear the restaurant at the top of the hill is great."

While we waited for a seat, I called Val's lawyer. He'd given the glove we found to the police, so I wasn't going to get a second look. The hostess came to lead us to a table just as my phone rang. I hated it when people took calls at the table, so I went back to the street to answer.

"Charity Deacon."

"You've been poking around my site again," Penelope snapped.

"How did you get my number?"

There was a pause then, "You gave me your card."

"I don't recall doing that." I knew I hadn't given her my card. Someone had given her my number, and it was probably a cop. "Why did you call?" Like I didn't know.

"You didn't take the hint when I complained to the police about your harassment. Perhaps you'll respond to a more direct action."

This was direct? "You can't stop me from trying to find the truth."

She laughed, and I got a chill. "I know some gentlemen who would disagree. What would make you stop?"

"I don't stop until I'm satisfied that the case is solved. Tell me, why are you so interested in pushing me off the case? Are you afraid of what I'll find?" My doubt about her was slipping away as she talked. The only reason I could think of for her to keep this going was guilt, or that someone Penelope cared for was the killer, and she was trying to protect them.

She laughed again. This time I thought it sounded a little strained. "I'm not afraid of you," she said. "I think we should meet. I can show you why you should stop."

Val stepped out and gave a questioning look. I pressed mute and told her to order me a chicken souvlaki. I took the phone off mute and said, "I'm not going to meet you, Penelope."

"Are you afraid?"

I'd been threatened by people better at this than her. "No. I'm busy. Is there a point to this call?"

"Yes, but I don't think you're getting it. Let me be plain. If you don't stop poking into where you aren't welcome, you will regret it."

Why did it feel like I was on the playground? If this bitch wanted to scare anyone, she'd need to take lessons. Now I was having serious second thoughts about her being a killer. She didn't seem to have it in her to be threatening. "Okay, your objections are noted." I disengaged and joined the others at the table.

It was great food, and an interesting view of the river and bridges. We were halfway through the meal and I was getting ready to start talking about our plans, when the waitress showed two men to the next table. They were a little too close for us to have a decent conversation about the case.

Val shrugged and said, "Hey, Rory, what are you doing about your documentary? I mean you're hanging out with us, and you can't film anything."

I stopped listening. I didn't like the way the two men were acting. Not talking. Leaning back as though they were listening to our conversation. They even waved the waitress away when she came to ask what they wanted. They gave me a creepy feeling, like they were watching us, even though they were staring out the window.

"Let's get back on the job," I said as I signaled for the bill. "I think we should take a step back and do some research on-line." The two men continued to ignore us until I'd paid the bill. When we headed for the door, I saw the closest man glance up and push his chair back.

"I don't know if digging around in the computer will help."

Val turned to look at me. She leaned in and whispered, "Hey, do you think those guys are following us?"

She'd gotten the same feeling I had. I gave her a gentle nudge. "Yes. Get outside fast."

When we were on the street, I looked around for a place to hide before the two lunks joined us. There was nothing promising, but the police station was only a couple of blocks away.

I needed to figure out who they were following. "Rory, can you head across the street and wait next door to the police station?" He didn't seem to understand why, but he nodded and dashed across the road. "Val, head down the hill with me. We'll split up at Fourth. You go join Rory, and I'll continue on. We'll see who they're interested in."

We started walking. I glanced over to see Rory lounging against the wall of the building, aiming what looked like a mini camera in our direction. A quick glance confirmed the two men trailing us.

"I think you should come with me," Val said. "It doesn't matter who they're following. We should tell the cops."

"No. It's not clear that they are following anyone and, what will we tell the cops? I won't let them get too close. You just join Rory. I'll be there in a few minutes. I promise."

We reached the corner, and she reluctantly did as I asked. I entered the Army & Navy, thinking that nothing would happen in a crowded store. When I got inside, I saw my mistake. No one was there. No customers, no employees. I knew there was an exit to Front Street downstairs, so I wouldn't have to turn around and ram into the thugs, if they were there.

I tried not to let my nerves get ahead of me. I needed to see if the two came in the store. I moved to a display of summer dresses and watched. They came in a few seconds later, looked around, and saw me.

Fear tightened my gut, but I moved slowly. There was no need to let them know I'd seem them and was scared.

They shadowed me down the stairs and I tried to lose them in the camping equipment department. I misjudged and they trapped me between the tent display and a stack of camp stoves. Still no witnesses.

"We aren't going to hurt you this time." This came from the one with a prison tattoo of a spider web covering his cheek and jaw. His voice sounded like it had been broken years ago. "This time, just a warning."

I met his gaze, and tried not to quaver when I said, "I'm not worried."

He grunted out a laugh and turned to his companion. "She thinks she's tough."

There was no response. Well, no spoken one. The guy's colleague just hunched his shoulders and flexed his biceps.

This wasn't the first time I'd been threatened with violence, but it didn't get easier to take. A real threat turns your organs cold. I'd felt it when Peter Wong had jumped into my car and put me in the hospital. I felt it now. They knew exactly how to use my own fears to do the job. No need to hit me when the terror of what they could do, would be just as useful. And if there was a camera in the store, it would look like we were just talking.

"What is the warning?" I asked, thinking I might was well get it over with. And speaking helped me to feel like I had some control of the outcome.

He leaned forward and poked a stubby finger at me. "Stay away from the building site. Stop asking questions about things you don't need to know. Go back to Vancouver."

I carefully tightened my muscles and kept my voice steady. "That's a lot of warning. Who sent you?" As if I didn't know.

"See, you should listen. That's a question about something you don't need to know." He loomed at me. "Do we need to make you listen?"

He didn't wait for an answer, just turned around, nodded at his partner, and lumbered out of my sight.

SIXTEEN

I waited until I was sure they weren't going to come back and then stepped into the aisle, keeping my focus on the stairs leading up to the main floor. The store was suddenly too hot. I had to get outside where I could run if the two goons came back at me. And I wasn't going down to Front Street. I needed to be on Columbia, close to the cop station, and on Rory's camera.

"Ma'am?"

My heart stopped, and I almost swung at the elderly man who appeared in front of me. Now there was a salesman? Where had he been two minutes ago?

"I'm sorry," he continued. "I didn't mean to startle you. Can I help you find something?"

I shook my head. I didn't want to talk because I was scared I would scream, or cry, all the tension from the two thugs jumping out of me. I had to tell myself he wasn't a threat; he was just doing his job.

"Well, if you are thinking of buying a tent, this one is on sale."

I shook my head still not ready to talk, but also not wanting to freak this guy out.

"If money doesn't matter, I can show you some top of the line products." He cocked his head and looked concerned. It was probably just concern over my customer experience, but I had to say something.

"I, uh, I was just looking. I have to go."

He shrugged. "Okay, if you're sure. Let me know if I can be of any help." He faded back past the racks of camping equipment.

I breathed out the tension from the adrenaline. I'd been okay with the actual threat, but the minute the thugs had gone, I was a wreck. What the hell was going on?

As I stepped through the door on to Columbia, I looked across at the cop station to see Val and Rory arguing. I waved to get their attention, and then jaywalked to join them.

"What happened?" Val asked.

"Let's go tell the cops." I didn't want to keep repeating the story. They could listen while I made my report. If Penelope was watching, she could just worry about what I was telling them.

Inside it was quieter than the last time I'd been in the station. The receptionist called someone right away. We were sitting in an office in front of Detective Reynolds before I'd had a chance to organize my story.

"Thanks for coming in so promptly, Ms. Deacon," Reynolds said.

What did he mean 'so promptly'? "I'm here to make a complaint."

Picking up his pen from the table, he asked, "What happened?"

I told him everything from the phone call to the threat. "I think the call was to stall me so the goons could get there."

He looked up from the pad where he was recording everything. "Do you have anything to support that theory?"

"No." I would get some, though.

He nodded and started making notes again. "Can you describe the two men, please?"

Rory passed me his phone. "We have them on video," I said as I pressed play and watched the two goons follow me into the store. Reynolds took the phone and replayed it.

"Can you send me the video?" He looked at Rory, not me, as he asked.

Rory took the phone and with a few taps sent it to Reynolds. The detective turned on his monitor. "Don't post that anywhere." He waited until Rory promised to keep the video offline. "Let me get this into the record. I'll need you to sign when I'm done."

I wasn't planning to just sit there quietly while he typed. "What are you going to do?"

He kept typing and answered without looking away from the screen. "These two are known to us. I'm going to bring them in for questioning. I don't hold out much hope they'll tell us who hired them. They're proud of their reputation as tough guys." He grabbed the mouse and clicked. A printer hummed to life on the counter behind him. He took the form and pushed it toward me. "Read it over and sign the bottom. If you need to change anything, let me know."

I glanced at what he'd printed. It was complete, not that the story was all that complex. I signed at the bottom and pushed it back. "Will you be asking Penelope Whitehall if she knows them?"

He gave me a disappointed look. "I know you don't think that we know how to do our job. I'm used to that from private investigators. I get it, we're the competition. Well we do want to solve these murders, and, despite your opinion, we do know what we're doing."

There wasn't much I could say to that. I wasn't going to give up on my investigation, but I wasn't going to get into a fight with the cops either. It didn't matter to me who found the killer as long as no one railroaded Val. "Okay. So, you thought we were here for something else."

"I left you a voicemail. We had to release our suspect because he has an alibi." He glanced at Val.

I put my hand on her arm to stop her from reacting. I was surprised when it worked. "What does that mean for my client?"

"We'll be rechecking her alibi, and we'll need you to stay available, Ms. Wei. We'll keep investigating all channels."

I'm sure he meant it to sound reasonable, but I didn't trust that they wouldn't go after her again. "So will we. If you have any questions for Val, please contact her lawyer."

"Understood. If you want my advice, Ms. Wei..." He waved off any response she might have had. "No, whether you want it or not, I'll give you this tip. Stay away from Ms. Whitehall. She's connected enough to get her way. If you push her too hard, it will come back to haunt the investigation."

"So, she's off the hook? What if she's the killer?" I knew Val well enough to hear the restraint in her voice. I worried that Reynolds would take it as belligerence.

"She's not off the hook, and if you have any concrete evidence that she could be responsible, I'll bring her in for questioning. Until then..."

Val slumped into the chair. "Yeah, well maybe we do."

"Val, let me deal with this." The glove was supposed to be in the cop's hands, but maybe it hadn't found its way to Detective Reynolds yet. "Val found a glove at the first murder site. Before you say anything, she knows that it was wrong to go in the crime scene."

"And what about giving the evidence to the police? Does

she know she should have done that?" The helpful tone was gone from his voice.

"We gave the glove to her lawyer. He told me he'd passed it along to you." I hoped I wasn't getting him into trouble.

"I haven't seen it yet. I'll check on it. So why does this glove implicate Ms. Whitehall?"

I explained about the uniqueness of the glove, and the link to Penelope.

"Okay. I'll follow up." He stood and we had no choice but to follow him.

He escorted us to the front lobby of the station and reminded us to keep out of the way of the official investigation and give them any clues we found. The words seemed conflicting, but maybe he was bowing to the inevitable.

Before I could tell Val and Rory what the next steps should be, Val's phone chirped. I don't know how people keep track of the different rings, but Val apparently had no problem. Her voice was all professional as she answered.

"Manage the Chaos. Val speaking. What can we organize for you today?"

She pulled a slip of paper from her pocket and dug around for a pencil while making listening noises. Rory presented his back as a desktop when Val looked for a hard surface. I saw a smile of appreciation flicker before she became serious again.

Tucking the phone between her ear and shoulder, Val said, "I can meet you today. What time works best?"

She scribbled a note. "Where do you want to meet?"

"Yes, I like to see the environment you need organizing so we can get a good idea of the extent of the project."

"Great, I'll see you there." She tapped the screen to disconnect. "Hey, Charity, I need to meet this new client in an hour. How about I go home and change. Then, when I'm done with my meeting, we can meet somewhere to get the investigation going."

I ignored the implication that I wouldn't be investigating unless she was with me. "Where are you meeting this person?"

"In his home. That's my thing, right? I go to people and help them at home, or the office."

"Babe." Rory dodged Val's punch. "Sorry, Val. Okay I'm not cool with you just going to a stranger's home. It could be dangerous."

Rebellion flashed across her face in a tightening of lips and narrowing of eyes. "I've been doing this alone for a while now. I don't need a babysitter."

I jumped in before Rory could push her too far. "Yes, but there haven't been murders going on, and you haven't been a suspect before. It makes sense to have a witness."

She relaxed a little. "I can't have Rory coming into the client's house dressed like he's some kind of gangsta wannabe. And there's no time for him to change." I opened my mouth to defend him. She held up a hand to silence me. "And I can't have a client thinking my mom needs to come along."

"Your mom? Do I look old enough to be your mom?"

She sighed. "Okay, maybe my older sister."

"Good." I wasn't happy to let Val go to the meeting alone, but I had make some calls that Val didn't need to sit through. "Where are you meeting this new client? What's his name?"

"Mr. Blackhouse. He's living down in Queen's Park. I can walk there easy, if I go and get changed now."

"How about Rory walks with you, and then waits outside. That way you aren't totally alone."

I could tell she was getting antsy to leave. "Look, I'll give you his address, and I promise I'll be careful. I don't want a chaperon. This is my business."

Rory shook his head. "Dude, if that's what you want, then it's okay. I don't agree with it, but it's your gig. I get it."

There wasn't much I could say to that. Since the goons had come after me, I figured Val was safe from Penelope, at least for a while. And she was right. I wouldn't want anyone telling me how to run my business either. She needed to feel like she could control her life. "I expect a call to confirm you're okay."

"Great. I might be a while. If the job looks promising, I usually spend some time looking around, so I can put a good price together."

I hoped her while wasn't more than a couple of hours. "Okay, by dinner then."

She agreed, and said she'd send me the details by text, before hurrying toward her apartment.

"Uh, Charity, what are we going to do next?" Rory hitched his backpack onto his shoulder and looked at me expectantly.

I didn't need a budding filmmaker around while I talked to Uncle Mike. He was happy to help me, but his past with the government had made him leery of exposure. He wouldn't even help Matthieu directly. I still think Uncle Mike's job was about more than public relations, like he claimed.

"Look, I need to do some work on my own. How about we meet for dinner. Val should be finished around then. I promise to call you when I hear from her."

He shrugged. "Sure. I'll do the same if she calls me first."

Optimism is a wonderful thing. "Can I drop you somewhere?"

"No, I have a car. I think I'll spend the day upgrading my wardrobe to a more Val approved state. You think that will help?"

He was hooked. I hoped Val was gentle with him if she decided not to get involved. "It couldn't hurt. Anyway, I think the movie business might require a bit less gangsta, and a bit more business, in directors."

"Truth."

I watched him head toward the parking lot, half hoping he would end up following Val regardless of her wishes. There was no way I was leaving New Westminster until Val sent me the details about this client.

After a few minutes, I started typing a reminder. Her text arrived just before I hit send. I wished her luck and started toward my car.

I saw something wrong as soon as I caught sight of it. The car was sitting too low on the ground. When I got to the parking space, I saw why. All four tires had been slashed, long gashes slicing the sides. They'd made sure I couldn't just patch the damage. Did they mean to tell me that this could be me next time?

My hand shook as I called roadside assistance to get the tires replaced, and as I disconnected, a thought hit me. They knew where I parked, and they knew which of the cars in this huge lot was mine.

I looked around, convinced that someone was going to lunge out and hurt me. I called roadside assistance back and told them I'd be waiting on Columbia and Fourth. A place where there would be witnesses in case I needed them.

SEVENTEEN

I reported the incident to the cops. Detective Reynolds told me there wasn't much they could do without video of someone committing the vandalism. He sounded sorry, but I'm not sure that he was. It took about an hour before I was able to leave, and almost a grand for the tires.

I drove home, constantly checking the cars around me. I didn't put my address on my business cards or website, so the only way the goons could find me was by following me. No cars appeared in my rear-view mirror more than a couple of times.

I felt much safer as soon as I closed and locked my front door. I'd been threatened here before, but it still felt like my home was a safe place to be.

Val hadn't called or texted, but I suspected she was going to hold out as long as she could, to teach everyone that she was capable of taking care of herself. Proving she was responsible enough to keep in touch would have been a better choice in my opinion, but I refrained from following up, mainly because she was right. She had taken care of herself in dangerous situations before.

I made a pot of tea, and then called Uncle Mike.

"Hi, kid, what's up?"

In the background, I heard laughter and jazz music. "It sounds like a party."

"Yep, I have a few buddies over. Don't worry, they can entertain themselves for a while. What can I do for you?"

Guilt pinched at me. "I do call you when I don't need something – occasionally."

He laughed. "Don't sweat it. I like helping out."

I believed him. At over eighty, he liked to keep busier than a man half his age. "I need to know how to do a deep background check on someone."

"You mean you need me to do it. Otherwise you'd have the information in your hands. Who is it?"

I gave him Penelope's information and everything Matthieu had managed to dig up. "We can't find anything older than five years online."

"I'll see what I can find. If she's in the program, I won't find anything, but that will tell us something. Give me an hour. If I can't find her within that, we'll need a new approach."

I thanked him and disconnected.

An hour with nothing to do but worry about Val and pace, didn't seem like a great idea. I checked the locks and the windows again, then took a shower and dressed in clean clothes. It felt like I washed away all the crappy stuff that happened today. I tossed a load of laundry in the washer and went downstairs to the kitchen. I was starving, and it was too early for dinner, but not too late for a big snack.

By the time I finished the last of the cottage cheese, I couldn't control the worry about Val any longer. I sent her a text asking how it was going and letting her know to come over for dinner. I waited but there was no reply. I sent Rory an invitation and directions to my place.

I tidied the first floor of the house. The benefit of living in a floating home was that it was so small you could clean it in less than an hour. The downside was that you couldn't hide any mess.

Mike phoned just as I was composing a new text to Val.

"I don't have much time. We've decided to move on to a club," he said by way of greeting.

I picked up my pen. "I'm ready."

"Okay, I've found a little more information, but not much. I did check with a buddy over in the RCMP, and he confirmed she's not in the program. He also couldn't find anything on her in their files. If she's hiding from something, it's not federal."

"Okay, I guess that's good news. We don't need to be bumping into official walls."

"I found her in Toronto about six years ago," he continued. "She was a real estate agent. There were a few best saleswoman awards, and one interesting thing. She had a listing in a shady area of downtown Toronto. She was showing it to a client when they found a dead body."

That was promising. "Murder?"

"Never really proven. The coroner closed the case as natural causes, but I've got a call into a friend on the force out there. If there was any question, she'll know."

Another dead end. "Anything else?"

"Yes. The client she was showing the property to was a well-known crime boss. I guess they need agents too. But if it was more than a business arrangement, she might be a good suspect."

I tried not to feel too excited, but no one touched that world without getting a stain on their fingers. "I knew there was something about her."

"Charity be careful. These guys are bad news."

I didn't tell him about being threatened. "I'll be careful." I made the promise, hoping I could keep it.

"I know you will. I also know you are stubborn enough to disregard risks when you think something is important."

He knew me too well. "It's not like they can find me unless I'm in their neighborhood."

There was a pause. "She's a realtor. It will be easy for her to find out where you live because you own the floating home."

I went cold. "I'll be extra careful." I might even move out for a while. "I'll let Jake know to be careful too. If they find out he's important to me, he'll be in danger."

"True. If you want me to keep digging, you'll need to get me some DNA, or at least fingerprints."

And if he kept digging, they might come after him. "No. I've got enough to go on. You stay out of it; I don't want you hurt."

He laughed. "I may be old, but I still know how to break a kneecap. I'm off. You be careful."

I promised again, but I knew we'd all be safer if I solved the case fast. Fast didn't usually mean careful.

EIGHTEEN

Val still hadn't called, and she wasn't responding to my texts either. I sent a text to Rory that dinner was canceled. He responded that it was cool because he was still shopping. If he was going to this much trouble to impress Val, he might just break through her self-reliant shell.

As much as I didn't want to run into the thugs again, I was going to have to go looking for Val. If she was just absorbed in a new job, I'd apologize for disturbing her and leave. I wouldn't be able to settle, or sleep, if I couldn't find her.

As I drove back to New Westminster, I considered calling Detective Reynolds, but at best, he'd tell me she wasn't gone long enough for them to investigate. At worst, he'd send out some uniforms to arrest her. I'd make it official if I didn't hear from her by tomorrow.

I was headed for the client's address, thinking that she wouldn't have gone home without letting me know.

The Queens Park area was close to Columbia Street, but it was miles away in atmosphere. The streets were quiet and residential. The houses were all old enough to have heritage status. Some had plaques on the wall that said just that. I pulled into an empty space a block away from the address I had on my phone and walked the tree-lined street. The shade was nice, but it didn't do anything to calm my worries.

The house Val's client lived in was one of the restored ones, dark green paint with cream detailing, they were heritage colors. The garden was a work in progress of dirt, and two shrubs that looked like they were dying. I knocked on the door and waited. I could hear a child screaming in fury, and a woman making placating sounds. Maybe Mrs. Blackhouse?

The door swung open to reveal a short woman about thirty, dark hair pulled into a braid, face red with frustration. "Yes?"

"Mrs. Blackhouse?"

"Yeah, what are you selling?"

Not a good time, obviously. "I'm not selling anything. I'm looking for someone. Val Wei?"

She glanced over her shoulder to where the toddler was lying on her back in the hallway screaming and kicking her feet. "I don't know a Val Wei. I'm kind of busy..."

Images of the worst-case scenarios started tightening my gut. "I see that. They can be a handful at that age. Val was coming here to meet with Mr. Blackhouse. Maybe he has a minute?"

"Mr. Blackhouse is in Hawaii at a convention. There's no way he was meeting anyone here today. Look, I've got to deal with this. I hope you find your friend. Leave me your card, I'll ask Alan about her when he calls later."

I handed over my card, but I didn't hold out much hope. Val's new client was a hoax, and I didn't have a clue what the connection was. If I could get the woman talking, maybe I'd learn something helpful. "I love the way you've restored this house. It's nice when people value the history of their homes."

"Thanks, but we didn't do it. The previous owner ran out of money and we got a great deal. I'm working on the garden in my spare time. We were lucky with our realtor. She had a reputation for finding deals like this."

The toddler had given up on the tantrum and was now peeking at me from behind her mother's legs. It gave me hope that I could keep Mrs. B talking. "Do you have her contact info? I might be in the market, if I can get something this nice."

She looked at my card. "Private Investigator?"

Half the people who asked that question were interested, and half were suspicious. She sounded suspicious. "Yes. I do lot of different kinds of investigations."

She put her hand on the child's head and looked down at her. "I'll send you the information on my realtor when I get a second. I have to go now."

I thanked her for her time and headed back to my car. I knew that there would be more to the email than realtor contact information. She had some secret she needed me to dig into. Not about the husband. If my instincts were working, it was something to do with the kid.

My instincts were also telling me it was time to report Val missing. I needed to do that in person because I needed to explain why they should take it seriously.

My car safely parked at a meter on Carnarvon Street, I made my way downhill to Columbia and turned right, and uphill. It felt like I was never going to walk on a flat street again.

I checked my phone, hoping that Val had sent a text, but no joy. I looked up as I put my phone away and almost walked into Penelope. She was looking through the window of a jewelry store.

I glanced in but didn't see anything special. "Looking for a new necklace?"

She twitched, and then glanced up to see my reflection in the glass. "Oh, you." She turned to face me. "I thought you were supposed to stay away from me."

It was a warning, not a restraining order. "It's a public street."

"Well, did you have something to say?"

"No. Just wondered what you were looking for." I figured it was as good a time as any to ask her a few questions. "I hear you used to work in Toronto."

"Yes. That's not a crime." She started to walk away.

I moved to block her. I needed to get this done fast. I was itching to get to the police. "It must have been awful to find that dead body."

I saw something ugly shining out of her eyes. "You've been investigating me? Do I have to talk to my lawyer to keep you away from me?"

"I'm looking into anyone connected with the case. You just turned out to be interesting. What happened in Toronto?"

"If you think I killed that man, you are wrong." There was fear in her voice.

What man was she referring to, the guy in Toronto, or one of the two bodies here? "Dead men do seem to surround you. Will I find any more if I look?"

She took a step toward me and clenched her fist. Maybe I had pushed her a little too far. I didn't step away, even though I could see how much she wanted to hit me.

Finally taking control, she said, "I haven't killed anyone. Leave me alone, or I will have you locked up for stalking me." She turned away and marched off.

I watched her go, and struggled with deciding to follow her, or go report Val missing. I settled on a compromise. I called the police while I started following her. When I got put on hold, I promised myself I wouldn't spend more than a half hour on Penelope. I just couldn't ignore this feeling she was involved in something. Maybe just a land scam, but something made her keep pushing me away harder than really necessary.

Keeping the phone to my ear while I listened to saccharine instrumental versions of old rock songs, I followed. She checked over her shoulder once, but I was ready and ducked into a used bookstore for a second.

She went into a cocktail bar, and I saw her meet a man at a table near the back. There was no away I could follow her without being seen, and they weren't near the window so I couldn't overhear what they were saying.

The music was still playing, making me wonder if my call had been shunted into limbo. I hung up and turned to head for the station. And there was Penelope.

"Now I know you're following me. Don't try to deny it."

"What are you talking about?" I'd learned that people could argue against a denial, but it was really hard to argue against innocence.

She sniffed. "You followed me here, and you're trying to slander me with councilman Peters."

So, she'd been meeting with politicians. That had all kinds of possibilities. Of course, not all of them would be suspect. "I don't know what you're talking about. I haven't talked to him."

She sniffed again and glanced over her shoulder. "Well, you can keep it that way. I need the connections I have in the council to be sweet. What do I have to do to make you go away?"

I couldn't ask her to prove she didn't kill Mr. Schell and Ken. I figured that would give her some ammunition to get me kicked off the investigation. Detective Reynolds wasn't being as obstructive as I expected, but it wouldn't take much to change that. "I'm just trying to figure out who killed these two people. Don't you want to find out who killed your employee?" It might have been wishful thinking on my part, but I thought she paled a little at the question.

"Of course." She checked her watch. "I gave the police the name of someone who might be a suspect."

"I know, but he had an alibi. What made you think he was a suspect?"

She paused, and I didn't think she would answer. I was getting antsy myself. It hadn't been that long, but I could hear the clock ticking on Val's disappearance.

Her gaze softened just a bit and then she nodded. "I saw that homeless man hanging around the building site. Ken had told him to move on. When the body was found, I wondered if the bum had gone off the deep end. I guess that wasn't fair of me to make the assumption, but the police took it seriously." She glanced at her watch again. "I have to be somewhere. Are you done with your interrogation?" The softness disappeared in a tightening of her facial muscles.

If she was in the mood to answer questions, I'd get in any I could. "Did Ken argue with anyone else?"

"Yes. He was arguing with the tattoo woman about some work she was doing. He told me he wasn't going to pay. And he was hard on the construction team as well. I have to go." She marched away before I could ask for more details. I hoped she wasn't heading off to give the thugs instructions on keeping me from bothering her.

I hurried to the cop station, all the while thinking that Ken didn't seem like the kind of person who would argue with anyone. The construction crew would be used to some rough language and demanding clients. They were more likely to down tools, and cause Penelope delays, than kill someone. Angelique, however, was connected to both murder victims. I would have sworn she was a good guy, but you never know.

I would check her out more after I reported Val missing.

NINETEEN

I glanced over at Ink & Needles, but the need to report Val missing was too strong. I couldn't justify any more delay. The shop would be there when I was done. Unlike Penelope, Angelique had been helpful. Although it didn't guarantee her innocence, it did make me feel that she could wait.

When I got to the police reception desk, I caught a glimpse of the back of one of the thugs as he was passing through the door to the back. There was no sign of his partner, so I could only hope that they were both locked in an interrogation room for a while. That did pose the problem, though. What if they saw me go into Detective Reynolds' office?

"Can I help you?" The receptionist asked before I could make up my mind to leave and do this over the phone.

"I'm here to see Detective Reynolds about a case."

She took my name and pointed me to a chair while she made a call. I watched her nod in response to something before hanging up. "He'll be out in a few minutes."

I picked up a magazine to keep my mind occupied. It was a new copy of some gossip tabloid. The picture of the celebrity on the front, had been mutilated by someone tearing the page. I couldn't concentrate on her high-profile problems. All I could do was juggle concern about Val and worry about the thugs. Were they here because of my complaint? Or had Penelope sent them to complain about me?

I checked my phone for texts again. Nothing from Val. One from Rory asking if she'd turned up. I replied that he shouldn't worry and slid the phone into my pocket.

"Ms. Deacon?" Detective Reynolds' voice cut through my thoughts.

I stood and walked toward him, but he held up his hand. "I don't think you want to go back there."

"I need to talk to you." I didn't want to blurt out that Val was missing in front of anyone who might walk into the waiting area.

"I need a coffee," he said. "You can talk to me at Starbucks."

We took a table in the back of the coffee shop and nudged the empty chairs away, so we had as much privacy as possible. My nerves were tight at the delay as we waited for our coffees to be called. It felt weird to be doing a police report outside the office. A bit too relaxed, and a bit too thoughtful of Detective Reynolds for me to believe he didn't have an agenda.

"Okay what do you have to tell me?" He took a notebook out of his jacket pocket and waited.

I had to clear my throat before I could start. Now that I wasn't investigating, it felt like Val had been gone for days not just a few hours. All the fears that I'd been denying rushed to the forefront, making it hard to talk without sobbing in a breath. "Val was supposed to call me hours ago, and she's not answering texts or calls. I know it's too early to declare her a missing person, but I thought that maybe since there is a murder, you'd make an exception." I stopped talking to take in a breath before I passed out.

Detective Reynolds frowned. "You should have come to me right away."

"I know. But she's an adult, and she's free to come and go as she pleases." The argument didn't ring true in my ears anymore, even though the logic was sound. "But I'm worried because she got a call to meet a new client and the woman at the address didn't know anything about it."

He flipped open the notebook and pulled a pen out of the wire spiral. "She's a person of interest in a murder investigation, so not really free to come and go. How do you know she didn't lie about the call?"

"She wouldn't lie to me." I didn't wait for him to react because I didn't need to turn this into an argument, and I needed him on my side. I swallowed and decided to try another approach. "I know that sounds weak, but Val is more likely to have told us to get lost than lie about a client. Especially since she knew I would check."

"I'll keep that in mind," he said.

I felt like I should try to make peace with him. I did owe him for not making me face the guys who had threatened me. "Thanks for not making me go to your office while the two thugs were there."

"I didn't want there to be any trouble. Now just tell me what happened with Miss Wei."

I gave him the details of Val's disappearance and he made notes. My coffee was cold by the time he'd finished with his questions. I checked my phone again, still no messages. "So, you'll look for her?"

He nodded. "I think she just took off. It's not like she has any ties, and she's under suspicion for a serious crime."

Everything he said made sense, but I knew Val wouldn't have promised to meet us if she was going to run. I couldn't believe she would hurt me like that again. "Yeah, but you'll look for her anyway, right?" I needed to hear him say it. I wasn't going to live with an assumption.

"Yes, we'll look for her. I just think we're better off starting with the bus stations." He stood and tossed his cup into the garbage. "Try to stay out of our way. I'll let you know when we find her." He left.

It was late, and I only had one thing I could do other than walk the streets hoping to find Val. I could go talk to Angelique.

I called and left one more voicemail for Val as I walked. It was about the twentieth message, and I tried to keep the panic out of my voice. "Please, Val. Call me. I need to know you're okay. The cops know you're missing and they're looking for you."

I ended the call when I reached Ink & Needles. It looked like it was closed, but the windows were darkened all the time. I guess no one wants to be watched as they got ink. The memory of Angelique's offer to tattoo me made me glance at the designs that were painted on the glass. Dragons, butterflies, and Chinese characters, but nothing called to me as something I would want to wear for eternity.

I pulled the handle. The door stuck. The sign beside it listed the hours of operation. Angelique should have been open for another half hour. There was a shade pulled down behind the door so that I couldn't see if anyone was inside.

I knocked, but there was no answer. Was Angelique missing? I shoved off the thought as paranoia. I'd already put her business number in my contact list, so I called and got her message. Family emergency, she'd be back tomorrow.

There were only a few people on the street, and I was feeling a bit exposed standing in front of the door. It was time to go home and do some research.

TWENTY

Val still hadn't called me back by the time I got home. I'd checked my phone at red lights until I got a text from Jake. Apparently, my notifications were working. I could stop the compulsive checking and concentrate on just worrying a hole in my stomach.

Jake invited me over for dinner. I decided it would be better than diving into some of the less official databases, while I didn't have a plan. He would be a good second opinion too. I needed a sounding board as much as I needed concrete information.

I stopped at my place long enough to brush my hair and change into a dress. Nothing fancy, but I didn't want to start taking Jake for granted. I put in a request for Val's phone records from a friend I had at her provider, then I picked up a bottle of wine from my rack and headed two doors down the finger dock to Jake's home. He opened the door and kissed me.

When I made it into his living room, I saw a plate of appetizers on his glass and metal coffee table. My stomach growled.

"When did you last eat something?" Jake took the wine from my hand and nudged me toward the couch. "Go ahead and start. I'll just get the rice going."

Jake loved to experiment in the kitchen. The joy he took in feeding people always amazed me, because I saw cooking as a chore. "What's for dinner?"

He answered from the kitchen. "Rice with adobo chicken thighs. Dessert is a surprise."

"I can wait to know what it is." I dipped some naan in a green sauce and tasted mint and a nice level of spice. "I miss seeing you around during the day."

He dropped beside me on the couch and handed me a glass of wine. "We're filming in North Van for the next couple of weeks. I won't see you much, long days. What's happening with your case?"

I sipped the wine before answering, "Val is missing."

He put his arm around me and hugged. "I know that must be hard for you. What happened?"

He listened, without comment, as I explained what I'd found. I could see the questions building up behind his calm expression. He was a great actor, but I knew him too well to take his silence as acceptance of my conclusions.

"So, now the cops are looking for Val, and Rory doesn't know she's missing, and I don't know what to do next," I said.

He went to the kitchen without speaking. When he came out, he held two plates and nodded toward his dining table. "Let's eat here."

I joined him and dug in. I really wanted him to tell me what he thought, but I was scared to hear that he didn't have any ideas.

He finally started talking when his plate was clean. "Why do you think you need to be involved?"

Not this again." Because I'm an investigator. Val needs me to help."

He shook his head. "No, she doesn't. She's quite capable of

taking care of herself, especially since she's no longer the prime suspect in the murder."

I wished he would just get it. "I know she can take care of herself in normal circumstances. This isn't normal."

He cleared the plates to the side and offered to fill my glass. When I shook my head, he continued. "Why her? I don't understand why you need to help her despite the fact that the cops are now doing a real investigation."

"She needs me." It sounded lame.

He looked intently at me. "No, you need her. It's like she's your sister. She's not. And she left you the last time you helped her."

"I don't need a sister," I answered. "She is just a client. Anyway, Val has a sister." As I said it I heard a voice in my head muttering, yeah, a sister who just abandons her.

"How do you know she hasn't just taken off again? How do you know she isn't just playing you?"

Dinner turned into a lump in my stomach. "Don't you mean how do I know she didn't kill those men?"

He held up a hand and shook his head. "I don't think she did that. I got to like her too, Charity. I just don't want you to be hurt when she goes away. Because she will. That's what she'd done up to now, maybe to survive, or maybe just out of habit."

He was overreacting. I'd been upset when Val took off last time, but I hadn't been suicidal. "I'm not going to give this up. She needs me."

He pressed his lips together. I couldn't tell if it was in disapproval, or acceptance. Instead of answering he cleared the dishes and asked if I wanted dessert.

"No. I'm not hungry." It felt like the food I'd already eaten was going to be a permanent fixture. "I won't get hurt. I know she's not my sister. I don't want to fight."

He came back to the table. "Me neither. We hardly see each

other these days. Okay, no fighting, but I will have a word with Val when she surfaces again. It's time she grew up and started treating people with some respect."

I hoped she'd get a chance to hear the lecture. I tried to ignore the worry that she was the latest victim. "We'll do that together."

He kissed me, and I felt we were safe again. "So, what do you do next?" he asked. "I mean if she's missing, and the cops are investigating the murders, what are you going to do?"

That was the question of the hour. "My number one priority is finding Val."

He nodded. "I figured. So, what's your next step? Can I do anything to help?"

"All I can think of is to go back to New West and follow any trail I can find."

"Alone? Can Matthieu help?"

"He's following up on another case. I can't pull him off. I'll be okay."

"What about that kid who was hanging around? The craft services kid."

"Rory. What about him? Do you think he knows where Val is?" I didn't think Rory was such a good liar that I wouldn't notice he was hiding something. But we'd only talked on the phone and texted since Val disappeared, so it just might be wishful thinking.

"No, I mean to help you. He was hot for Val, so maybe he knows something that will help you find her."

It was worth a try. I knew Jake would offer to come with me, but he had an early call on set and the last time he'd tried to help me with an investigation it hadn't gone well. He'd lost a part in a long running TV show.

I wasn't crazy about doing this on my own either. Rory might be good cover too. "I'll give him a call. And I think I'll pass on dessert. I just had an idea where Val might be." If she was hiding, she might go to her street friends, or her home.

Jake pulled me up from the chair and into a hug. "Be safe, Charity. I don't want to have to come looking for you."

I kissed him long and hard before pulling away and heading back to my house.

TWENTY-ONE

When I called Rory, there was a lot of background noise, so I got straight to the point. "Hi, have you heard from Val?"

"Charity? Hang on, dude." The noise dwindled, so I assumed he was leaving a party. "That's better. My mom is having some people over. What did you say?"

"I asked if you'd heard from Val. She hasn't called me, and I'm worried."

"Nope, I didn't expect to, though. Do you mean she never called you after that interview? Like, she's been missing for almost a whole day?" His voice got higher as he continued. "Dude, we have to find her. What if she's in danger?"

I tried to keep the panic out of my voice, but it was hard when his was evident. "I'm sure it's just something that came up. I was going to look around for her."

"In New West? I'll meet you there. I'll bring my camera, and I'll keep a record of everything. It will be like an episode of Homicide Investigations. When we find her, it will be a great scene." He hesitated. "We will find her, right?"

"Of course we will." He didn't argue, so either he was happy to hope I was telling the truth, or I was a better liar than I thought. "Where in New West."

"I can take transit. What about meeting me outside the Columbia Street station? I can be there in about half an hour." His words came out in a rush. Like he wasn't giving me a chance to say no.

"It might be dangerous," I said. I didn't want him to run into this with his eyes closed. Infatuation can do weird things to young people – and maybe not so young ones.

"Dude, if it's dangerous, you're gonna need a wingman."

I laughed. If nothing else, he would keep me from freaking out. "Dress in dark clothes. I'm not sure where we'll need to go." I hung up and took my own clothing advice. Dark clothes helped if you were going to be skulking around, and they didn't hurt if you weren't.

RORY WAS ALREADY WAITING when I pulled up in front of the Skytrain station. His backpack slung over his shoulder; he was lounging against the wall. I parked on the street and we headed for Val's home.

Rory strode beside me on the almost empty street. "If she's there and not answering, I'll be pissed off. Is she like that?"

I remembered how she was impossible to get away from when we were looking for her sister. "No, in fact, the opposite. If she's there, you'll have to wait your turn. I promise to leave you something to yell about."

He looked at me and quirked his mouth in a half smile. "I wouldn't get between you and her at the best of times. What's the deal with you two?"

"No deal."

"Okay, I get it."

I didn't press on what he got. It wasn't important.

Val wasn't home. We knocked, and then I picked the lock. Just in case she was in trouble and couldn't get to the door, or shout out, or was too deeply asleep to hear us.

No sign of her.

The neighbor to the right was home with the stereo turned up full volume. That couldn't be the way they left the radio when they went out, so I knocked as hard as I could, and we waited. After a few minutes, I knocked again. The volume of the music diminished and when the door opened, I was surprised to see a woman who looked to be in her late sixties.

"Yes?" She didn't seem to be happy to be interrupted in the middle of a gangsta rap album. "Well, what do you want?"

I introduced us, and then asked about Val when it became obvious we weren't going to get her name. The woman's scowl turned into a smile. "I haven't seen her for a couple of days. Is she okay?"

It seemed that Val could make friends with anyone she ran across. Of course, I guess that would be if she wanted to. "I'm sure she is. Do you know her well?"

"Only to say hi. She's a good neighbor. Never complains about anything. Never gives me cause to complain." She glanced at the door. "Sometimes, I can't even tell if she's home or not."

That was a good example of life in a city if I ever heard one. "Do you have any idea where she might be at this time of night?"

The woman raised an eyebrow. "Well, she did like to help the unfortunates on the street. I know she would go down and feed them of an evening. I sometimes give her sandwiches, or fruit, to take." She checked her watch. "Oh, it's very late, perhaps she's finished that now."

I should have thought about that and gone there first. Even at one am she might be helping the homeless people. "Thanks, that helps. I'm sorry we disturbed you." I turned away to see Rory with camera held at hip level. The neighbor wouldn't have seen it, and I was still blocking her view. I glared at Rory and he grinned back. Sliding the camera into his pocket, he winked. "Excuse me, ma'am. I like your music. Who is it?"

I turned to see the woman shrug. "My nephew gave it to me. He knows I like some hard sounds in background when I work."

"Oh, what kind of work?" Rory was showing promise as an investigator. He knew how to build a rapport before interrogation. Something that felt to me like a waste of time right now.

"I'm an artist. I'm currently creating a piece of wall art for the new community center." She glanced behind her. "I don't like to show people my work in progress."

I touched Rory on the shoulder and gave a gentle push to turn him away. "I can understand that. I think we should get on our way. Thanks for talking to us."

"Wait," she said. "Do you think Val is in trouble?"

I told her about the murders but kept it factual.

"Well, that might explain something," she said, dragging her hands through her hair making it stand on end. "I get so involved in a project, I often haven't a clue what's going on around me. Val said she gets the same way when she works with her clients. She offered to help me get organized once. But I think chaos feeds the creative spirit, don't you?"

Maybe the paint fumes were addling her a little. "I'm sure you are right. You were going to tell us something..."

She frowned. "Oh, yes. I get so involved in my projects that an earthquake wouldn't pull me out of the groove. But there was something yesterday. It brought me out, and I realized I needed to eat."

I nodded and prompted her again.

"Well, there was some banging on Val's door. It sounded like someone was trying to break in. I looked through the peep-hole and saw two rather brutish looking men banging on her door. I was going to call the police, but they left while I watched. I was going to let Val know the next time I saw her." She looked over her shoulder again. "I really must get back to work."

She didn't wait for us to acknowledge the information, just turned back to the apartment, and locked the door behind her.

Our next stop was on Front Street where the dark doorways and alcoves held huddled bundles of humanity and rags. Rory had his camera out but kept it discreet. We were doing our best to get a response from people who really didn't want to be bothered. I had a bunch of five dollar bills available. I didn't mind giving some money to street people. I just preferred to give it to the organizations that helped them.

TWO HOURS LATER, all we'd manage to get were a collection of lies and fantasies. There were some people who just mumbled and turned over in their coverings. A man and woman conspired together to try to get more money from us before they gave us any information. I walked away rather than pay for what was going to be another bundle of lies. One man was convinced we were aliens come to take him to our home planet. He was eager to come but had no idea who Val was.

I was getting pretty discouraged, along with tired, cold, and hungry. "Rory, do you have any idea how to get some answers?" I don't know why I thought he might be better at this than me, but it was worth a try.

"I guess I thought people would be more interested in helping someone who helped them. Man, I would have been wasting my time if I just came down and started filming a documentary." He looked around before putting his camera in his backpack. "These guys are hardcore."

"I guess everyone has a right to be left alone." Despite what I said, I didn't want to accept the fact that no one would talk about Val. Were they so far gone that they didn't feel any gratitude for what she'd been doing? "Maybe we need to do something nice. If Val hasn't been around, they might be hungry. We can get some sandwiches and trade food for information."

He frowned. "Dude, that sounds mean."

"I didn't mean we would withhold food." I know that's what it sounded like. "I meant, if we feed the people here, maybe they would be more likely to talk."

There weren't any restaurants open at three am, but I knew there was a 24-hour Macdonald's nearby.

It took about fifteen minutes, and a hundred bucks, to get back with food. In the meantime, people seemed to have woken up. There was a huddle of them near the building lot. When we approached with the bags of food, one of the men stepped away from the group and came toward us.

He held his hand out for the bags. "Word got around. Food always brings people out of their sleeping spots." He had an English accent and his voice was soft. "And I see you've put your camera away. Good move."

I passed the food over and introduced myself and Rory. "We're trying to find out where Val Wei might be. She's been missing for hours."

He put the food next to the group of people and took a burger before coming back to answer. "Thanks for this. Val usually comes by earlier. I was worried about her."

Rory stepped forward with his hand out to shake. "Are you Brummie?"

He just looked at the hand and took another bite. "Yep."

Rory self-consciously dropped his arm. "I'm glad the police let you go."

"They had nothing on me."

I took out one of my cards. "Val is a friend, and I'm worried she's in big trouble. Have you seen her?"

Brummie didn't take my card. "You think maybe she'll be the next body?"

My heart stopped. It was bad enough that I was worried about that, but to hear someone say the words seemed to give them life. "I'm trying not to think about that."

"Who are you to Val anyway? How do I know you are a friend? Maybe you and Martin Scorsese here are doing these murders."

This was going nowhere. We would be better off waiting for the phone records I'd requested than asking her 'friends' to help. "I don't have any way of proving I'm not a killer, so I guess we'll go. Enjoy the food, I'm sure Val will show up soon so you can get your next meal." It came out as mean as I felt it. Being down on your luck wasn't an excuse for being so unconcerned about people.

Rory took my card and held it out to Brummie again. "Look, you don't really think we're the bad guys. Why would we bring food and ask about Val if we were going to kill her? You guys would totally be able to identify us. Take the card. If you think of anything, or change your mind about helping, give Charity a call."

Before Brummie could say anything, Rory took my arm and made me walk away.

I was impressed with his tact. "We could have tried to talk to someone else."

"No, that dude was the leader. If he won't talk, the others won't either. Maybe he'll call, but we won't get anywhere sticking around."

"How do you know so much about how this works?"

He laughed. "Man, you've been away from high school too long. Unless you're part of the in crowd, you need to learn about group dynamics to survive. Anyway, I want to be a documentary director, so I do research on things. Now what's next?"

TWENTY-TWO

"Lady!" Brummie called before I could come up with an answer. He was hurrying down the block we'd put between us and the building site. "Wait."

Rory smiled at me and got his camera ready.

When Brummie reached us, he put his hands on his knees and gasped for breath. It was hard to believe that someone would be so winded after running a single block, but it was probably a long time since he'd had a healthy meal and a full night's rest.

When he had his breathing under control, he started talking, "One of the guys told me something. He didn't want to get into trouble with the cops. I don't know what kind of trouble he's expecting. We don't ask down here. I won't tell you his name."

He paused as if waiting for agreement before giving us vital information. I pulled out my notebook and pen. "I won't ask. Just tell me what you know."

He narrowed his eyes and stared at me then turned to Rory. "Turn that off."

I followed Brummie's glance. Rory was looking at the screen of his camera finger poised over the stop button.

"Dude, I promise I won't use anything without your permission."

"I won't give it." Brummie's stance changed slightly. He seemed to get bigger, and he definitely got more aggressive.

"Look, dude. Having this filmed means Charity doesn't have to rely on her notes. You want us to find Val, right? Then make it easier. Let me keep recording." His face was a portrait of innocence.

Brummie glared but seemed to be thinking over what Rory had said. "How do I know I won't end up on Facebook, or something? I don't want people finding me."

The way he said people made me think it was something like the Russian mob, or the CIA. It was like he was spitting the word out to get rid of the taste. I held out my hand for the camera. "I'll keep it in my pocket. Will that do?"

Brummie nodded, and I dropped the camera into my jacket pocket without turning it off. No picture, but we'd have sound. Rory was right. A recording was better than my scratched notes.

I held the notebook and pen ready to take down his information. "Okay, Brummie, tell us what you have."

He stared at my pocket then shrugged. "One of the guys. He saw Val yesterday. He hangs out at Queen's Park during the day. Anyway, Bra- I mean this guy could tell she was mad at something. She was walking along poking at her phone. She didn't even see him, which is unusual because she always sees us and says hi, and, if she has some food with her, she just gives it. She doesn't give us money. She doesn't trust us to spend it on food. She's right."

He ran out of steam. For a second I thought he was angling for some cash. I agreed with Val. I didn't want to be responsible for someone's drug habit.

It seemed he was just regaining his train of thought. "What was I talking about?"

"Someone saw Val yesterday." I kept my voice even. He didn't need to know that the guy he was talking about was probably the last person to see Val.

"Oh, yeah. So, my friend was going to get up and say hi, just to be friendly. But before he could, a car pulled up alongside Val. And he couldn't see what happened. The car was between him and Val, right? Okay, so he heard some yelling, but he couldn't tell what they were yelling about. And he could only hear Val." He suddenly looked around as though expecting the 'people' he feared to jump out from behind one of the pillars holding up the parking structure.

I had a million questions but he was on a roll so I let him keep going. Rory was letting me control the conversation, even though I could feel him almost vibrating with the need to do something.

Brummie shook himself and started talking again, "Anyway, Val stopped yelling and got in the car." He stopped like he'd run out of words.

Time for questions. "Did he see if she got in voluntarily?"

"I thought of that too. He said she didn't yell, or anything. But I figured she might have been drugged, and then she couldn't yell, right." He started to shuffle his feet, and then looked around again.

I needed to calm him down. "There's no one else here, Brummie."

"You don't know that!" His agitation was increasing with every minute.

"Okay only a few more questions. Did your friend describe the car?"

"Yeah, a newer one, sliver, and low to the road. He didn't get a license plate, before you ask. He might have gotten one, but he doesn't remember it."

Disappointing, but maybe the police could make more of this than I could. "Would he be able to recognize the car?"

Brummie looked around again, this time the panic on his face was clear.

"Brummie, will your friend talk to the police?" I knew the cops wouldn't get much headway with just hearsay.

"No! No cops!" His fists clenched, and he stopped looking at me to stare at a darkened doorway.

The conversation was going to be over if I couldn't find a way to distract him from his private hell. The problem was I needed to talk to his friend, and that meant building more trust. I needed more time, and we didn't have any.

Rory stepped forward. "Look, dude. There's no one there. I can prove it." He moved toward the doorway.

Brummie's hand shot out and pulled him back.

"They know how to hide," he hissed. "Don't go in there, or they'll have you, and you'll forget everything you know."

Rory pulled his arm from Brummie's grasp. "Okay. Thanks for saving my life, dude."

"You both be careful." Brummie seemed a little calmer.

Rory leaned in and said, "You know, dude, it would be better if we talked directly to your buddy. Why don't you just take us to him?"

Brummie's face drained of all color. His eyes widened, and he started to shake all over. "They got you! No! Go away." He shuffled backwards as though afraid to turn his back on us. "They got Val, and now they got you." He turned and ran back toward the building site shouting as he did.

I pulled the camera out of my pocket and handed it back to Rory.

"Sorry, Charity. I shouldn't have asked that," he said.

"It's not your fault. He was feeling his demons before you said anything." I glanced toward the doorway. "He did see someone there, you know. I just wonder if the whole thing about Val was the same kind of hallucination."

We took the information to the police station where a young constable listened to the recording. He added the new information to the file and informed us that Detective Reynolds would be on duty in a few hours.

He added, "There's not much to go on, Ms. Deacon."

"I know, but it's more than we had before. I don't suppose you'll give me any details on the suspects in the murder cases. Like, what kind of cars they drive." I'd learned in my short career that the only thing you got when you didn't ask questions was silence.

"No," the constable answered as he shut the computer file. "You need to leave this to us. I'm sure your friend will show up with a good explanation."

I wasn't mean enough to ask him for the basis of his optimism. "Has there been any progress on the murders?"

"I can't tell you that either. And I think you know that." He stood and started to escort us to the door.

Rory held the door for me, and then started asking questions while he was in the doorway.

"Have there been any other murders?" I'm not sure why he thought the question needed to be asked while we were standing at the open door.

The cop thought for a moment, and then seemed to dismiss the danger of leaking information to a civilian. "No and I hope there won't be any more."

"Me too. I don't want to find my girlfriend in the morgue." He held up the camera. "Do you have anything you want to make sure gets into the movie?"

As the constable stepped forward to take the camera, Rory

stepped through to the street and let the door go. "Nope, you can't have this."

Joining us on the street the cop leaned in close. "Don't get in our way. You may think you have some kind of freedom of the press thing going on, but I can get a warrant for the camera. You've already told me it contains information that might be pertinent to an open case."

Rory stood his ground. "Yeah, you can get a warrant, but you won't. You know everything we know. Maybe the New West Police would like to be on record in a positive way when the movie hits the internet."

Save me from young men who feel the need to own their territory. "Okay, that's enough. Officer, we're leaving. If we learn anything else, I'll send the information to Detective Reynolds." I pulled Rory by the elbow to make him back away. "Rory, we need to eat and figure out what we do next."

With a little distance, the tension left both men. Rory made a show of turning the camera off and dropping it into his pocket. "Fine, I know a place we can go."

THE PLACE TURNED out to be an excellent all-night diner in Burnaby, only ten minutes away. We ordered breakfast and coffee and sat in silence until the food arrived. I was trying to figure out what would be the most valuable thing to do to save Val. I'm not sure what Rory was thinking.

"Here you go." The waiter slid our plates in front of us and asked if we wanted more coffee. I declined. The acid was starting to eat a hole in my stomach. Rory nodded.

There's something about being hungry that shuts down any higher-level thinking. The need for food becomes paramount. I dipped toast in the egg yolks and watched the rest ooze deliciously toward my bacon and pancakes.

I looked up and saw Rory shoveling hash into his mouth, barely chewing between forkfuls. I got heartburn just watching. "You'll regret that in about a half hour. Slow down. There's no rush. We need to talk before we do anything else."

He stopped with his fork buried in the mound of food on his plate. "Aren't we going to try and trace the cars? Don't you have some private investigator database?"

I wish. "Nope. I do have access to some databases, but when I need information I have to rely on friends. People who work at the insurance company, and the phone company."

"You have someone at ICBC? Cool, can you get some points pulled off my license?"

I laughed and poured syrup on my pancakes. "No. Learn to drive better."

"I figured." He grinned at me. "So, what do we do until you can talk to your friends?"

That was the question. "I think Val is okay. I mean, I don't think she's totally okay, but whoever took her hasn't killed her yet, or someone would have found the body. I think we let the cops deal with that for a while."

"How long is a while?" He pushed the remaining food on his plate to the side. "I don't know her well, but I'm kind of crushing on Val. If she's hurt, and we could have done something, I don't know how I would deal."

He wasn't the only one. But I had enough experience with finding information to know when to take a break. "If we had any clue to follow, we would be on it. I won't let the cops hang around on this. If they don't get anywhere in the first couple of hours, we'll go back and start pressuring them."

"Okay."

Waiting didn't sit well with me either. "What we can do is try to solve the murders. I don't have much more on that, but I do have one clue that might be new."

He perked up. Pulling his camera out, he held it at shoulder height – I was glad it was just a little one that didn't attract the attention of any other diner. Rory started asking questions. "What exactly is the clue?"

I held up my hand. "Put the camera away. I'm not putting this person on the record as being a suspect. We're off the record until we're sure."

He made sure I could see the camera was off before tucking it into his backpack. "Okay, but can we make this investigation my first real movie?"

"What do you mean by movie?" I'd seen how much it took to capture a movie for release. When Jake worked, there were at least ten cameras, and lighting, and makeup, and special microphones, and an army of people whose jobs were unclear.

"It's for the internet. I've got a plan. I'll put a couple of movies up on YouTube. Some producers will see them, and I'll get funded."

I had no idea if it would work, but at least he had some direction. "It's a plan. I promise I'll help you get this one into shape for uploading. But you have to make sure no one can be identified unless you have permission. And you won't get mine."

He shrugged. "I get it. A private investigator needs to be low profile, right?"

I nodded, that would be as good an excuse as any. "I need to do some research on this person. I think you need some sleep. How about we meet again at eleven am?"

"I could help you with the research." He stifled a yawn.

"Nope, you need some sleep, and so do I. Otherwise we won't be thinking straight." Even a few hours would help.

I paid the bill and offered to drive Rory home. "It's still too early for transit to be running. And I think you live too far to walk."

Instead of answering, he asked a question. "Who is the suspect?"

I reminded myself that he was kind of my partner in this case. "I got this from an unreliable source, but the woman who runs the tattoo parlor."

Surprise brightened his face. "Angelique? I guess it's possible. She's a weird one. I asked if she would let me film an ink job, and she got this weird look in her eyes. Then she said she'd ask a client."

I tried not to read too much into the 'weird one' comment. "So where am I dropping you off?"

He agreed to let me drive him to Broadway and Clark, insisting that he only lived a block away. I didn't press it. He must have a home somewhere, because he didn't look like he was homeless. Maybe he just wasn't comfortable with people knowing where he lived.

TWENTY-THREE

By the time I got back to New West, I was feeling refreshed from a two-hour sleep, courtesy of a mug of herbal tea. It had been hard to settle, but I knew that I'd be more use to Val if I didn't keep pushing myself to the limit.

A call to Matthieu had assured me that all the other cases we had were moving along. He'd done some research into Angelique, but not much since she wasn't a suspect.

"Everyone connected to the crime is a suspect at the beginning, Charity." He'd reminded me when I asked why he'd dug into her background. His experience as a cop came in handy. My usual case didn't require me to find the suspects. They were identified by the client.

He suggested I start with credit records, a database I had legitimate access to, because I paid a rather large fee every year to maintain my membership.

I put my car into the stall and hoped the hulks didn't decide to slash my tires again. The only alternative was to find parking on the street, and that would take time that I didn't want to waste.

Rory was leaning against a store window. He hadn't noticed

me, so I had a chance to check him out for a minute. He looked like he'd slept. Unfortunately, it was in the clothes he'd been wearing. If he wanted to be part of Val's life, he would need to smarten up. I reminded myself that was up to Val, not me. I wasn't in a position to judge her boyfriends.

I called his name as I got close and his head snapped in my direction. If I didn't think it was crazy, I would have sworn he was napping. How could he sleep with all these people around?

"Hey, is there any news?" He didn't sound hopeful.

"Not about Val. But I have some interesting information on Angelique." I pulled out my notebook. "She's only had financial records for the last five years." Just like Penelope.

"Whoa, does that mean she might be in witness protection? Maybe she's some gangster's chick, and she informed on him. Maybe these murdered dudes got in the way of some kind of revenge."

That kind of imagination would do him well in the movie industry, but as an investigator, I was more inclined to ask questions than make up stories. "It could mean anything, including the fact that she just didn't need loans, or bank accounts, until then. But I agree it is weird." I showed him the list of credit card and bank accounts that I'd noted. "Let me do the talking."

"Can I film?" He hoisted the backpack onto his shoulder.

"Only if you do it discreetly. We don't want to scare her off." I stepped beside him as we headed to Ink & Needles. "When we've questioned Angelique, we'll go ask Detective Reynolds what's happening with Val's case. Maybe he has a lead we can follow."

He spent the short walk to the tattoo parlor fumbling with the settings on his camera.

The store was open this time.

We entered the showroom and waited while an overly muscled man picked through a catalog. It wasn't Angelique

behind the counter. It was a guy who looked to be in his twen-
ties until you saw the gray streaks in his otherwise black ponytail. That didn't mean she wasn't in the back.

When the customer finished booking his appointment, we
were alone with the tattoo artist.

"Hi, do you know what you want done?" He glanced from
me to Rory. "A matching symbol?"

"We're not looking for ink right now. Is Angelique around?"
I handed him my business card.

Looking at it, the artist shook his head. "I haven't heard from
her since yesterday." He held out my card to return it. "What
would a private investigator need with her?"

"Can I have your name?" It felt weird not to know who I
was talking to.

"You can call me Jude." He nodded toward Rory. "Who's
your sidekick?"

"I'm not her sidekick, dude." He stepped forward with a
card of his own. "Rory Macdonald, director."

"Director, huh? Would I have seen any of your stuff?" I
couldn't tell if he was actually interested or whether he was
calling Rory on the reality of being a director.

"Nothing in theaters, yet. My YouTube channel is on my
card. Check it out."

I'd had enough of the chit chat. Rory could make fans when
we found Val. "So, do you know where we might find
Angelique?"

Jude started clearing binders from the counter. He didn't
look at us as he spoke, "She's pretty private. I only work here a
couple of days a week. Sometimes she takes off without telling
me. I have a key, so I can open up if she's not around."

That didn't answer my question.

"Dude, you know there's been some murders, right?" Rory

seemed to have forgotten agreeing to let me do the talking, but I let him take the lead anyway.

Jude looked up. "I heard. The travel agent guy, and some real estate agent. So?" His sudden focus on us contrasted with the insouciance of his tone.

Rory leaned forward, angry. "So? So, maybe Angelique is the next victim. Or maybe if we find her, we can stop her from becoming the next victim." He calmed down before continuing. "I'm sure she'll be cool. We're not the cops."

Jude reached under the counter for something. I braced myself in case he pulled out a weapon. I relaxed at the sight of an address book. An old fashioned one with tabs for the letters of the alphabet.

"Here's her cell number. She doesn't keep her address on file. I think she's afraid of someone finding her. But I know she lives in that apartment building by the river, the one close to the water."

"How do you know?" It didn't make sense that Angelique would keep her address private and yet tell an employee, or whatever Jude was, where she lived.

"I was down there one afternoon. I saw her go into the building. She didn't have to buzz the intercom, so I figured she lived there."

After getting a clearer description of the apartment building, we left.

We followed Jude's advice and took the market overpass. The community on the quay was separated from the rest of New Westminster by a high-traffic railroad system. For pedestrians, there were only two ways in that didn't run the risk of up to twenty minutes waiting for a train to pass. The market was a good place to enter the neighborhood, but the building we needed was at the other end of the boardwalk.

We picked up coffees and started the walk along the river.

This was a bit like where I lived, but instead of one street of floating homes, this was high density living at its best. The mix of three-story townhouses and condo towers left a feeling of openness that balanced with the river which was busy with tugboats.

"What if she isn't home?" Rory was taking panoramic shots of the river. "I mean, do we keep looking, or do we go to the cops?"

"We'll keep looking for her for a while. Unlike Val's case, the cops would need more than just the fact that Angelique was missing for a while to go looking for her." Maybe she was in bed sick after the family emergency.

"These shots will be a great contrast to the desperation of the street people." He took one more picture then sped up to pass me. "This must be it."

The main entrance was on the other side of the building. We'd taken the boardwalk because Jude suggested it. He thought our chances of running into Angelique, if she was out for a walk, were higher if we went that way.

When we got to the front of the building, I found A. Roman on the Enterphone and buzzed. When she didn't answer, I buzzed again, and again. There was no doubt she was away. I called her cell phone again, no voicemail. It sure seemed like she didn't want to be contacted. I called Jude just in case Angelique had been in touch. No luck. I turned to Rory. Sometimes it helps to have a fresh mind on the problem. "Any ideas?"

He didn't answer and I turned to see him staring intently at his phone.

"Rory?"

He looked up. "Hey. I was just checking to see if she was on anything like Facebook or Twitter."

I didn't think there was a good chance of that, since she was trying to keep herself as private as possible while still running a business. "What did you find?"

"There's a Facebook page for Ink & Needles." He held up his phone to show me.

"I thought you needed to have a personal page for that." I didn't have a business page for that reason.

"Yeah, it's under the name of Tatchick, but there's no personal information available." He flicked through some postings. "She was at a party last night. Looks like they are trashing the place."

There were a few postings about a party at a house not far from where we were. Angelique had been the star demolition expert by the comments on the post. "Okay, it's worth a look. I think we need the car."

TWENTY-FOUR

There was no sign of life at the house when we arrived. It was probably too much to expect that Angelique would answer the door, since we were lucky enough to actually get the address from the Facebook event.

"Maybe they should have just 'dozed it." Rory stood beside me on the sidewalk. The house was barely standing. A demo party didn't usually mean pulling down the house, just doing some internal demolishing. It was hard to see what anyone could salvage from the mess around us.

I checked out the lock on the gate. The padlock was broken. "Okay, be careful where you walk. I don't want to have to explain to Val how I broke you."

"You think she'll care?" He held up his hand to stop me from answering, even though I hadn't planned on it. "Hang on, dude. I want to set this up." He leaned his backpack against a pile of rubble and then placed his camera on a tripod. When he was satisfied, Rory walked back a few steps, keeping his eyes on the display. "Okay, Charity. Will you come into the shot? I'll ask you a couple of questions about the investigation."

When had I agreed to be on camera? "Only two questions, then we need to get inside and look around."

He pointed me to a spot where I'd be in the best position for the camera. Then he got me to pull my hair into a ponytail. Taking a microphone from his pocket, he cleared his throat. "Ms. Deacon, can you explain to the viewer what we're trying to accomplish here."

"As you know, we are in the middle of an investigation into two murders. We got involved because the police accused a friend of the first murder, and now that friend has gone missing."

He nodded and gave me an encouraging smile. "And what do you think we'll find here?"

Great questions. He was going to make good documentaries. "We're following a clue that might help the police solve the case. I'm hoping it will lead to some clue about the missing person. We have to be careful how we act. We need to help the police, rather than get in their way."

He thanked me and turned off the microphone. "Okay let me get the camera."

I walked confidently up to the open wall at the top of the steps. If anyone was watching, I hoped they got the impression we were authorized to be there.

Inside, the first floor was a mess of broken tiles and drywall. I turned to Rory. "Look for anything people may have dropped."

He panned the camera across the mess and then put it away. We dug around for a while, but after ten minutes of poking into the piles of broken house, we didn't find anything.

"What about the second floor?" Rory asked bringing out the camera and turning it on the stairs. "Should we go up?"

I'd lost my confidence in finding anything here. In the Facebook pictures, people were drinking beer from bottles and plastic cups. There were pizza boxes and bag of chips in the background. Today there wasn't a sign of anything like that. Someone had done a great cleanup of the evidence.

"I'm not sure how safe it is. We should—"

"I'll go first." He started up the stairs testing each tread as he went. "The stairs are good. Come up. I'll check the bedrooms."

"Rory, wait for me." I carefully followed his path using the sides of the stairs rather than the center. He wasn't there when I got to the top of the stairs. I looked into the first of the two rooms off a small landing.

"There's nothing in here," Rory said crossing to the other room. The door was intact and closed. Rory opened it and a cloud of flies bloomed out. "Oh, crap."

I could tell by the smell that followed the flies what was in the room. I pushed past him digging out my phone. "Are you going to be sick?"

He turned to face me, pale, but not panicky. "No, I'll be okay." He scrambled for the camera. "I can't be squeamish if I'm going to make great documentaries."

He was right, but I admired his control. I'd seen a few bodies, and I still felt my stomach rebel. "Good, keep your camera running and step backwards to the landing. You don't want to mess up the scene any more than you already have."

I looked at Angelique's body as I followed him. She was laid out so that we could see the slit in her throat, flies were landing on the flesh. I pressed my lips together to stop the urge to gag. Someone had cut her throat and left her to bleed out onto the hardwood floors.

It took the cops five minutes to arrive. They worked fast. Two went upstairs to secure the body and the third officer separated me and Rory before taking our statements.

The medical examiner arrived right before Detective Reynolds pulled up.

TWENTY-FIVE

We were taken to the police station in separate cars. I saw Rory being escorted into an interview room on the opposite side from me. Then I was put in the other room. Four walls, no windows, a camera in the far corner of the ceiling, a metal table, and two chairs were the only other items to look at.

I wasn't left alone very long. Detective Reynolds opened the door and sat across from me. "You know we're recording this. I need to ask you some questions about what you found."

I didn't have anything to hide. "Okay, let's get started. When you've got your answers, I want to know what you are doing to find Val." I knew I should ask for a lawyer, but that would just delay things. I hoped Rory was careful about what he said, but there was nothing I could do to help him right away. When I'd told him not to talk, he'd grunted something I didn't catch.

"Tell me how you came to be in the house." He sat back in the chair, relaxed relying on the camera to take the notes. Or maybe there was someone listening who would take them for him.

I gave him the facts. "So, what are you doing to find Val?"

"Not so fast. What made you think Angelique Roman was a suspect in the murders?"

"Penelope Whitehall gave me her name." I watched to see if that surprised him.

He didn't react. "Why didn't you tell me, rather than just run off and find a body?"

"I assumed she'd already given you the name. You should probably ask her why she didn't. She's not very forthcoming with information, but she always seems to have something when pushed."

He shook his head in disbelief. "Have you ever known someone who negotiates for a living come out with all the facts without reason?"

"Two, no three, murders isn't enough reason?" Why wasn't he bringing Penelope in for questioning?

"Good point. Now, when you learned Ms. Roman was missing why didn't you come to us?"

He wasn't going to be distracted. "It wasn't clear that she was missing. I don't know her well enough to know if she was acting out of character."

He leaned in toward me. "Where were you last night around three am?"

"I was trying to find Val Wei. I reported some new information. Did you get the update?"

He shook his head. "Not yet. I got called out on a murder before I could catch up on new information on my cases. Is there a reason Ms. Roman would have your business card?"

Maybe I should call a lawyer. "Am I a suspect?"

"We need to ask these questions. You must know that." He looked at me waiting for an answer.

I considered calling Lu to get me a lawyer, but I hadn't done anything, so I kept talking. "I gave it to her a couple of days ago.

She was going to find some information for me on the Schell murder."

"There four calls from an unknown number on her phone. Will we find them on yours?"

I pulled my phone out and unlocked it. "Check for yourself. I made a couple of calls today. She didn't have voicemail, so I couldn't connect."

He flipped through my call log. "You could have gotten a throwaway."

"I didn't, but you know I can't prove it. Look if I'm a suspect, tell me now, or I'm leaving."

"Right now, everyone is a suspect. Do you have any information that will lead us to the killer?"

I felt like we were playing a tug-o-war over information, and I was losing. "I don't know her that well. Check with the other tattoo artist. He said his name was Jude."

"We are checking. The young man with you when we arrived, what do you know about him?"

I wasn't going to be tricked into getting Rory into trouble, but the facts wouldn't hurt. "He was working the craft table at the movie shoot. He is attracted to Val and helping me with the case because he wants to find her. And he wants to make documentaries. I don't think he had anything to do with this, he was with me. Anything else?"

Before Detective Reynolds could ask me any other questions, someone knocked on the door. When it opened, a man dressed for golf stood in the doorway. "I'd like a moment with my client, please."

Reynolds looked pissed. "MacDonald, who called you?"

"That's irrelevant. Both of my clients are here. I want a word with this one." He held the door open.

Reynolds stood, pulled a remote from his pocket, and turned off the camera. "Let me know when you're done."

I didn't have a chance to speak before I was alone in the room with one of Vancouver's most well-known lawyers; Rance Macdonald. "Why are you here?"

He smiled and held out his hand. "My son asked me to make sure you were okay before we left."

I shook his hand and asked, "Your son?"

"Rory. I guess he didn't tell you who his father was." He shrugged. "Happens all the time. He doesn't like living in the shadow of my reputation. I can't blame him. I don't like it either."

"Wait a minute, you're Rory's father?" Two more different people probably didn't exist in any family.

"Yep. Let's get down to business. Have you been charged with anything?"

"No. They don't have anything to hold me on, and I don't think Reynolds thinks I'm a real suspect." I couldn't let Rance Macdonald get involved, and in my way. "I can't afford you."

"Pro bono. You are helping Rory. I'll help you."

I was going to have to talk to Rory about honesty. I'm not sure how Val was going to react when she found out. "Okay, look, I don't want to antagonize the cops here. I need them to let me work on the murders, and I need them to help me find Val."

He nodded and smiled. "That's the girl who Rory keeps talking about. She's missing?"

"Has been for almost a day. I know that's not long, but someone is tangling her in these murders, and that worries me."

He glanced at the camera; it was still off. "Okay. I'll get them to release you. If they think you're a suspect, it might not work. But we'll try to do this civilized."

"What about Rory?"

He checked his watch. "He's waiting for me in the reception area. They had nothing to keep him on. At least they don't now. He was ready to fight over giving them the camera."

We agreed he would do all the talking until I was released. Mr. Macdonald opened the door and invited Detective Reynolds back into the room.

When we were settled, me sitting, both men lounging against the wall, Rance started talking. "My client is ready to assist in the investigation."

Detective Reynolds moved away from the wall and put my phone on the table. I hadn't noticed that he took it with him. "We don't have any more questions at this time. Your client needs to be available if we have any in the future."

"Agreed."

I felt like an ornament in the room. The two men were bargaining over my freedom. I had to actually bite my cheek to stop from interrupting.

Reynolds continued. "And we need to have all the information she has on the three murders."

MacDonald looked at me, eyebrow raised.

Time for the client to speak, I guess. "I don't have anything more to give you."

Reynolds nodded. "Then you are free to go."

Macdonald held up a hand to stop me from standing. I was starting to understand two things, why he was so highly regarded, and why Rory wanted distance.

"You had my client's phone. Do you have any other belongings that you shouldn't have? Of either client."

Reynolds pulled the door open. "No. I have to get back to my cases."

I jumped up. "Wait. What about Val. Have you followed any of the leads?"

Reynolds gestured for me to leave. "Not yet, but I promise we're looking. I don't want another body found on my watch. This case, and I mean the murders and Val Wei missing, is top priority."

TWENTY-SIX

We found Rory sitting on a chair in the lobby when we entered. He stood, held out his hand to his father, and said, "Thank you." He sounded cold and there was no gratitude in his voice.

I watched the man's reaction. He definitely looked disappointed, but I wasn't sure if it was at the offer of a handshake, or just at his son.

He shook the hand. "I'll get back to my foursome."

I thanked Rance and waited until the door closed behind him. "Rory, why didn't you say who your father was?"

He looked at the ground. "I don't like it when people think I'm trading on his name. Anyway, why does it matter?"

He had a point. I didn't press him, but I remembered dropping him off in East Vancouver. He'd done more than just omit the fact that he was Rance Macdonald's son. He'd activity lied. "I suggest you come clean to Val when she shows up." I wondered how his dad would feel about Val's history.

He shrugged. The nonchalance was betrayed by the flush that flooded his cheeks. "I guess. Anyway, what are the cops doing to find her? Is this new murder taking their attention?"

I glanced at the front desk. "That's what we're going to find out. They told us she was a priority, but I want to know more than that before we leave." I walked up to the reception desk and looked for a bell, or something to summon someone. I didn't see anything, which didn't make sense. How would they know if someone was waiting out here?

I checked the ceiling for cameras and found one that covered the whole area. I stared up and waited. After a few seconds, Detective Reynolds opened the door behind the reception desk. "What more do you want?"

I tried to look helpful, a smile pasted on my face. "I want to know what I can do to help you find Val and solve the murders."

He narrowed his eyes. "Your lawyer won't like me talking to you."

I kept the smile firmly in place. "Unless you plan to arrest me, it doesn't matter what Rance Macdonald likes."

He looked at Rory. "The kid stays here. I'm not taking on the Macdonald's."

I turned to see Rory checking his camera. I'd expected them to confiscate it, but I guess his dad made an arrangement. "Rory, wait here, okay?"

"But I need the footage."

I patted his arm. "It's complicated."

He looked like he was going to argue, but his shoulders slumped instead. "See why I don't tell people who my dad is?"

I felt bad for him. He was right. No matter what he wanted, a famous dad would always be part of the equation. "It's not fair, I know. But will you wait?"

"Yeah. I want to find Val as much as you do, even if I can't get it on film." He sat and started checking something on his phone.

I thanked him. I wanted to give him a hug, but I let it lie and followed Detective Reynolds to his desk.

"Okay. I've had a chance to read your report. It's not much, and this Brummie isn't a great source of information."

I didn't want to hear the problems. "He seemed okay most of the time. Are you going to do something?"

"Yes. We'll bring him in again and see if we can get him to tell us about the car he saw." He sounded reluctant.

"You mean the car his buddy saw."

Reynolds shook his head. "Nope. Brummie was in the park. He does that, pretends someone else does this stuff. We might find that his details are off too. He likes to inject a little drama."

I should have noticed that. I was letting my worry for Val interfere with the investigation. "Okay, what can I do to help?"

He flipped his file open. "Val has a sister, right? Can you contact her?"

"No. Do you think Val went to Emma?" I didn't think so, but maybe we could track her down.

He looked at me as though I was stupid. "Don't you think it's a possibility? I mean her sister is the only family she has, right?"

"Yes, but they aren't close." I changed the subject. "Can I be here when you talk to Brummie?"

He shook his head. "That won't be a good idea."

I had to keep trying. "I thought you agreed to let me help."

He pushed the file toward me. "Take a look at the file and tell me if there's anything you can do better than us. In fact," he said pulling a thicker file from a drawer, "here's the murder investigation. Take a look there too. Maybe you can find something we've missed."

There was no sarcasm in his voice, but I couldn't believe he was letting me see the files. "Are you kidding?"

He opened the top folder. "I was when I started, but now I'm desperate. Take a look."

I wasn't going to ask again and risk him changing his mind.

Starting with Val's file, I looked through the forms and pictures. I didn't have anything to add. "Can I make notes?"

"No."

"If this were my case, I think I'd be pursuing Brummie. You guys are probably way more qualified to do that than me."

"Wow, slow down. I don't know if I can restrain my ego."

"Very funny." I pulled the murder file toward me. This one took much longer to review. I did my best to memorize some new facts that I found, mostly background material on the key suspects. I skipped over my own sheet. They'd done a good job of investigating everyone who was a suspect, including Val. There were three sheets with names on the top and nothing else.

I looked up to see Reynolds watching me like he could read my mind. "Why are these three people on the list?"

He took the forms from me. "Okay this guy had a fight with Ken Leeman about the way he was dealing with the developments. We followed up, and he's been out of the country in the time period we know the murders were committed. This one is Mr. Schell's ex-wife. She doesn't have a motive. He was generous in the divorce and paid the alimony on time. She's not in getting anything in the will. I've got the notes separately, and we'll fill out the official documents when we close the case." He pointed to a sheet with Penelope Whitehall's name on top. "And this one, we haven't gotten much on her. She was a low priority suspect."

"Who gave you the leads to the other suspects?" I knew that the minute I gave him what I knew about Penelope, my chance to get information would be gone.

"The ex-wife was a standard procedure. We got three of the other suspects from Ms. Whitehall. She's pretty connected right now, so she's been helpful."

Helpful enough to be under the radar on the suspect list. "So, she's a suspect, too. Why?"

He pushed the documents around. "She's also connected to two of the murders. I don't know if there's any connection to the Roman case, yet."

I pulled out my phone and opened the file I'd made on Penelope. "I've done some background checks on her. I'll send you the file." While I pretended to fumble with sending the file, I took some pictures of the contents of the folder on the table.

Reynolds checked his computer and thanked me for the information. "I'll get someone to verify this. Now, is there anything else?"

"Penelope told me that Angelique had fought with Mr. Schell. I don't know if that helps or not, now that Angelique is dead."

He made a note before standing and escorting me out of the office.

Rory was waiting for me when Reynolds shooed me through the door. The receptionist was back in her chair and talking to an older woman who was clearly upset about something.

I beckoned Rory to follow me because I wasn't going to talk inside, where anyone could be listening.

"I need coffee," I said, drawing him into the Starbucks. "What can I get you?"

"I'll take a double shot of espresso. Are we staying for a while?"

I placed our orders before answering. "No. I've got an idea to run past you."

"Okay. So, maybe, we should eat something while you do that." He eyed the sandwiches on display.

I checked my phone for the time, and realized we were about an hour past lunch. "Good idea." I added two cookies and a couple of sandwiches to the order.

Rory found us a seat at the counter facing the street. I brought the coffee and cookies. He jumped up to get our sandwiches when they were called.

After chomping through half his sandwich, he said, "Okay, dude. What's the idea?"

I hoped it sounded less desperate to him than it did in my head. "The cops will do a better job of following up on the clues they have than we can. And in finding Val." That hurt to admit. "Reynolds let me look at their files on both cases. When I was talking to him about it, I realized there was one person involved in almost every aspect of both cases."

He looked troubled. "I don't want to forget about Val. Can we let the cops do the murder investigation?"

"We've done all we can, Rory. I'm out of ideas." His face reflected my feelings. It hurt to let the cops take over. I couldn't quiet the little voice that told me she wasn't a priority, because she wasn't the only suspect. But I really had run out of ideas.

He rubbed his face, and I saw how young he really was when he looked back at me. His eyes held that same look a kid has when they realize the grown up is right. I hated the fact that I was the grown up here.

"Okay, but if I find out something about Val, we follow it, right?"

"How are you going to find information on Val?" If he had some real resources, then I would take advantage.

"I don't know. Maybe one of the street people will trust me. Anyway, what did the detective think about your info?"

"He said he'd get on it, but I already had more information on this than the police." And I didn't think they were planning on following up soon on my information.

He swallowed the last bite of sandwich. "I did learn some stuff from my dad and withholding information from the cops is not a great idea."

Smart kid. "I sent Reynolds the information, don't fret. So, the idea is we follow this person around, and hope we see something that leads us to Val, or the murderer, or both." It sounded pretty lame to me. I was supposed to be the private investigator. I shouldn't be asking him for approval. Rory didn't seem to notice.

"So, who is it? And why are you keeping it a secret."

I looked around. "It's Penelope Whitehall, and I don't want to let anyone know what we're planning."

"Whoa, you mean the woman who complained about you when you weren't doing anything wrong? And the one who probably sent those thugs after you? And the one that Val thinks is the murderer?" He nodded slowly. I thought it was in approval of my bad-assedness, but it could be in wonder at my stupidity.

"Yes. So, you can see why I don't want her to know what I'm planning."

He took the bags from our sandwiches and cookies and tossed them in the trash. I hadn't even noticed I'd eaten anything.

When he got back, Rory started asking questions, "Okay so, what do I do to help?"

"We need to split up so it's less obvious that we're following her. We'll take turns."

"What happens if we see anything?"

I wasn't planning on any big take downs. "We call the cops. No heroics."

He looked out to the street like he was starting surveillance. "What happens if she takes off in a car?"

No plan was perfect. "We hope she doesn't, but if she does, at least we'll find out what car she's driving."

"Can we put a bug on her car? So we can follow her with a GPS or something?" He looked hopeful.

Good idea, but I was going to have to keep him grounded in the possible. "I don't have that equipment."

He picked up his backpack, and I half expected him to pull out a tracker and tell me about an app. "Okay, what do we do first?"

TWENTY-SEVEN

The first place to look was obvious, the development office. Thinking it would be better that Penelope didn't see me, I sent Rory in to see if she was there. His cover was easy. He was scouting for locations for a movie. We did the phone thing, so I could hear what went on.

"Hey, I was hoping to talk to the woman in charge." A little blunt, but movie people tended to be all business, so it might be fine.

I heard a muffled reply. The voice could have been a man, or a deep voiced woman.

"Do you know when she'll be back?"

A mumble.

"Okay, dude. Don't be like that. I'll come back later."

Rory joined me on the side street a minute later.

"She's at a meeting somewhere. The guy didn't know where, or how long she'd be gone."

"You did fine. We won't just hang around here. I'll call her and pretend I'm interested in buying something." It was a long shot that she'd believe me. "She won't pass up a potential sale. Or rather a realtor wouldn't pass up a potential sale, and it will mean something if she doesn't want to meet with me. In the meantime, let's see if we can get into that club."

There were very few people on the streets and none of them were loitering. If we could find a way to get into the nightclub, it was a good time to do it. We hurried to the front door, but that was too public. The building was on the corner of the block. I peeked around the corner and saw a door on the side that might offer a little more privacy.

"Are you going to pick the lock?" Rory asked.

"Yes, but I won't teach you." It wasn't exactly legal for me to pick locks, but I had a good excuse – it might not help, but being an investigator sometimes bought me some slack. Rory, looking the way he did, wouldn't get a word out before they put him in cuffs. It wouldn't matter who his father was until after he was in jail.

Rory leaned against the building keeping watch while I picked the lock. It wasn't a complicated one, so we were inside within a minute. We were in the service area of the nightclub. I flicked on the light, and saw a kitchen ahead, and a closed door to the left about halfway down. "Do you have a flashlight?" I asked, pulling my own from my purse. Rory dug around and retrieved a small one.

I turned off the lights, just in case someone came to prep for the evening, and we made our way to the door. It was locked. I had Rory aim his penlight at the lock and picked it. This one was newer than the one on the exterior door. It gave me some confidence that there was something worth protecting behind it.

Opening the door, we found a staircase that led to a low basement. The room at the bottom was fairly large, and open. If this was a sex club, it was one that didn't value privacy. We surveyed the space, which was empty. The two side walls had brackets bolted into the concrete.

"Dude," Rory said. "I don't want to know what goes on here. Is there anything we can use?"

I was disappointed, but not surprised, that we hadn't found any clues. "If we have good reason to think anything went on here, we'll tell the cops. Maybe there's DNA they can use." I didn't want to think what kind of bodily fluids they'd find – or where they'd find them.

We made our way back to the street. The interior door was self-locking. The exterior one just needed me to press a button to lock it as we stepped onto the street. "Okay, I guess we'll cross that off the list."

My phone buzzed. It was Matthieu. It could wait.

"Maybe you should get that." Rory was looking over my shoulder. "Maybe he found something."

"He's been working other cases. I'll just let it go to voice-mail." As I said it, I felt guilty. He'd been carrying the entire caseload, so I could concentrate on this. I slid the bar to accept the call. "Hi, Matthieu."

"Charity, you must come to emergency."

My heart stopped. Who was in emergency? "Which one?"

"The St Paul's hospital. I am in the waiting area. How long will it take you to arrive?" His voice was measured. Not calm but held in check.

I looked to my car and then at the traffic, as though it was going to help me assess the travel time. I closed my eyes and got a grip on my panic. "I'll be a half hour at least. How bad are you hurt?"

"Not me. It is Val. She came to your house. I was there doing some work. She is badly beaten. She will be fine, but you should be here, I think."

I grabbed Rory's arm and started running to the car. "How did she get to the house?"

"She arrived in a taxi. I do not know why the driver didn't take her to the hospital."

"We're on our way." I ended the call and told Rory, "Val's back and she's been hurt. Matthieu took her to the hospital."

He started running faster, and now he was leading me. "Will you be okay to drive? Maybe we should do transit?"

I dug my keys out as we made the final run to the car. "No. We can't take the chance that it will breakdown. I need to be driving." I couldn't imagine sitting on the Skytrain waiting to get downtown. At least if I was driving, I'd feel like I was doing something.

Rory snapped his seatbelt closed as I pulled out of the spot. "Should we call the cops?" he asked.

I pulled out my phone, unlocked it, and tossed it to him. "Reynolds' direct line is in there."

Rory passed on the information to the detective as I negotiated the traffic toward the highway. "Reynolds has some questions."

"Shoot." We'd made it to the highway in record time. I pulled into the fast lane and pressed the gas pedal to the floor. The traffic was light. There was no guarantee it would stay that way, so I was taking advantage while I could get some speed.

"No, not from you. He wants Matthieu's number."

I rattled it off. "I doubt he'll get anything more than we have, but maybe they will communicate better, cop to cop."

He ended the call with Reynolds. "Matthieu's a cop?"

The traffic was starting to get heavier. I pulled around a semi and sped past. "He was, in France. He quit and came here."

"Man, you are connected to a bunch of really cool stories." He looked out of the window.

I dodged around another semi. "I'm connected to people, Rory. You'll do better if you remember that."

"Yeah, yeah, I get it. My dad tells me that I get too excited about the story and forget the people."

We'd arrived in the city and I had to slow down. "Your dad is a smart man."

We drove in silence for five minutes and then Rory said, "Maybe I should call him."

We were at a red light, so I took my attention off the road and looked at him. "I don't think anyone is in trouble with the law."

He blushed. "No. I mean, maybe, he, uh... he's good with emergency situations."

So, Rory wanted his dad there if Val was in really bad shape. He needed his dad, regardless of what he said. Maybe they would advance to a hug rather than a handshake. "Tell him we'll be there in about ten minutes."

He pulled out his phone. "Where?"

I realized I hadn't given him any details other than that Val was hurt. "St. Paul's."

Rory called, but he hung up without saying anything.

"Why did you change your mind?"

"Oh, voicemail. I'll call him later. Maybe I should tell Val who I am before she gets the full Rance treatment." He looked out of the window for the rest of the ride.

TWENTY-EIGHT

As far as I could tell, Rory was still trying to figure out how to deal with telling Val about his family when we walked into the ER. I saw Matthieu before he noticed us. He was sitting in one of the plastic chairs, flipping through something on a tablet. Worry had aged him a decade in the last couple of days.

I didn't understand how Val wormed her way into our hearts, but she was lodged firmly in our family. Even the people who were angry about how she'd hurt me, cared about her. And it wasn't because a young girl had been beaten, although that was bad enough. It was because Val had been beaten.

Matthieu glanced up and noticed us. "Ah, good. You are here just at the right time. Val has been moved to a bed. She will have a chance to rest without the noise of the emergency ward."

I swallowed a sudden lump in my chest. Now that I didn't have to concentrate on driving, the emotions were threatening to take over. I reminded myself that I'd be no use to Val if I broke down. "How bad is she?" I clenched my hands to stop them from shaking.

Matthieu looked over my shoulder. "Who is this?"

I'd been with Rory for so long, it didn't seem possible that he hadn't met everyone I knew. I introduced him, leaving out his family connections, and added, "He's been helping with the investigation."

Matthieu pursed his lips, suddenly all French policeman. "It can be helpful to work with someone. I have told you this before, Charity."

Ignoring the dig at my need to work alone, I repeated my question, "How bad?"

"She will be fine. They are keeping her in overnight just to be sure." He drew me toward the hallway. "Come, we will see if she is still awake."

It took a few minutes to get to the room. The whole walk I felt the weight of illness settle onto my shoulders. My face began to ache with the memory of the beating that put me in this same hospital when I first met Val.

"Sir, how bad does she look?" Rory's voice was quiet.

Matthieu pressed the elevator button. "She has some bruises on her face. I think, perhaps, she is hurt elsewhere, but she will recover, young man."

Rory straightened and ran his hand over his face. "Okay, I just wanted to be prepped, right? Like I didn't want to wince or something and make her feel worse."

I gave his shoulder a squeeze. "I don't think she'll care. Just be nice and don't press her."

When we got to the ward, I saw four beds. Two were empty, one had a sleeping woman, and the final one held Val. She was sitting up against the pillows, facing away from us, poking at the bed controls. The head of the bed was rising, but she wasn't placed well, and she slid down as the angle got steeper.

I grabbed a stool from the corner of the ward. "It will be easier if you don't try to turn it into a chair."

She turned to face me, and I winced. She had a black eye, and her lip was split. There was a bruise shading her jaw. She slumped against the pillows and mumbled, "I was hoping you'd be alone."

Rory moved past me. "Dude, what did you do to the other guy?" He kissed her gently on an unbruised patch of skin. "I hope he's in the morgue."

Val tried to smile, but the pain in her lips stopped it at a grimace. I knew that feeling. She was fighting pain and exhaustion. It was time to get the facts, then let her rest. "Val, who did this?"

"I don't know. I didn't see a face. It was mostly one guy. He was slim, but he wore a mask and gloves. The guy who picked me up was there too."

Matthieu pulled up a second stool. "I didn't ask any questions. She needs rest, I think."

I wasn't sure how much rest she would get. A beating like that caused more than physical damage. I tried not to think about what she saw when she shut her eyes. When it had happened to me, I could see the fist coming at me. I knew that Val wouldn't want me to linger over feeling sorry for her. I couldn't stop it, but I could pretend I didn't feel the anger and guilt that weighed on me at the sight of her face. We needed information now before the cops arrived and took over. "How did you get away?"

"I didn't get away. They let me go. At least, I think so." There was no fight in her voice, and she didn't shrug Rory off when he took her hand.

"What?" I reached for my notebook, but then noticed Matthieu was already scribbling. "Why would they let you go?"

"I don't know, but before they did someone else showed up. I heard them arguing. No, that's not quite right. I heard the guys who did this arguing. I didn't hear the other person."

I nodded. She might remember something more helpful

given more time, but we couldn't leave the cops out of it much longer.

Rory patted her hand. "Dude, I thought you were going to be body number four. I'm glad you aren't"

Matthieu looked up from his notes. "Number four? There has been another death?"

I brought him up to date while watching Val's reaction.

She looked out the window. "I liked Angelique, that's too bad. We need to find this killer, Charity."

I promised we would, and then said, "You need to talk to the police."

I watched the argument flash across her face and then resignation settled. "I know. Will you stay with me? When they come, I mean. I don't want to be alone with them."

Rory glanced at me. I gave him a quick nod. "Of course, we'll all stay. Let me go call the detective."

I gestured to Matthieu to join me in the cell phone allowed area. As we left, I heard Rory tell Val he had something to tell her.

"Why do we both need to call in the authorities?" Matthieu asked.

I pulled out my phone and called Detective Reynolds. When Reynolds answered the call, I told him Val's ward number. He said he wasn't that far away. I ended the call, and then answered Matthieu's question. "Rory isn't the poor aspiring documentary filmmaker he makes himself out to be."

He glanced over my shoulder and tensed. I knew he wanted to barge back into the room and make sure Val was all right. "He is not making films?"

I shook my head. "No. I mean, yes he's making films, but he's not poor. His father is a well-known lawyer. He needs to tell Val, and I'm not sure if Val's going to appreciate the deception."

"I worry that you are correct. That young lady needs some stability in her life. And, perhaps, having a lawyer connected to her will come in handy."

"You think the cops will suspect her still?"

He shrugged. "I don't know. But I sense she's always going to be rubbing people in authority the wrong way."

I couldn't argue with that. We went back to the ward to wait for Reynolds to arrive.

TWENTY-NINE

When he arrived, Reynolds did his best to get rid of us. When we didn't take the hint, he finally came out and said, "I need to talk to Ms. Wei alone."

Rory held Val's hand. "I think I should call my dad. Val's been hurt and you shouldn't be making her worse."

Reynolds looked to me as though expecting me to take his side. I wasn't going to abandon her. "Does she need a lawyer?"

He sighed and pulled out his notebook. "No. Just let me get the story down before Ms. Wei falls asleep."

Nice, like it was our fault she was being kept awake. I nodded to him.

"Val, are you feeling up to answering some questions?" he asked, suddenly all concerned.

"Yes. Ask away." Her eyelids fluttered.

"Tell me what happened."

Val shifted a little higher in the bed and let go of Rory's hand. "I went to meet a new client, but the woman didn't know anything about it. Then I was going to call Charity, to meet her, but some guy pulled up in a car."

"Can you describe the guy?"

"He was maybe in his thirties. Not too old, but not my age. He had short brown hair and stubble, like he hadn't shaved in a couple of days. Before you ask, nothing that would make him stick out in a crowd."

Reynolds nodded but kept his eyes on Val. "Okay. What did he say to get you into the car?"

Her eyelids had been closing, but his words snapped her back to consciousness. "Yeah, I should have known better, right?" A bit of her old spunk broke through the pain medication and exhaustion.

"No, but he must have done something to convince you." Reynolds wasn't taking the bait.

She made an effort to keep her eyes focused on him. "He said he was from the client. That there was a mix up in the address. I don't know why I believed him."

Reynolds put his pen down. "Don't try to figure it out, Ms. Wei. You seem like a smart girl. You made a judgment, and you used all the information you had at hand. Blaming yourself doesn't help." He looked at me. "Maybe it will be easier for her if you aren't here."

Val jerked upright. "No. I don't want her to leave."

He nodded and held up a hand to placate her. "Okay, but you need to talk to me without worrying about what people think."

Val looked at Rory and Matthieu, then down at the hand Rory was holding. I saw her give him a squeeze before saying. "Do you guys mind waiting outside?"

Rory looked like he was going to argue, but Matthieu beckoned to him. "Come, we can get some coffee. You can tell me about your movies."

As they left, I moved to Val's bedside and settled onto the stool. "Okay, let's hear it." I hoped it wasn't rape or, or I don't know what. The beating was bad enough.

She started twisting the sheet between her fingers. "I guess I was kind of hoping for more work, and I let my brain check out."

Reynolds started writing again. "Okay, don't blame yourself. What happened after you got in the car?"

She reached for my hand. "He started driving, and I asked him where we were going. I guess I started to get suspicious. Anyway, he said it wasn't far, and then I felt something stick in my arm."

"Did he do that?"

She rubbed her arm. "No. It was like there was a pin in the back of the seat. Anyway, the next thing I know I'm in a dark room tied to a chair. Then someone comes in, but I didn't see who, because they didn't turn on the lights. Then they started beating me up."

"No one asked any questions?" Reynolds asked.

Val blinked back tears. Her voice small, she continued, "Not until later. I don't know how long it was, but they left, and then came back and beat me again. Then they came back after a while and told me that I should stop poking into things I don't understand."

He made notes. "Did they say anything specific?"

She regained a bit of energy now that she'd told him the facts. "No. But I'm guessing it has to do with the murders. It's not like I'm investigating anything else."

Reynolds flattened his lips. I could feel the annoyance rising off him. "Then what happened?"

"Someone came, and then they left me alone for a long time. It was still dark, and I hurt a lot, but I managed to wiggle out of the ropes. And then I just left."

"Then you left? What do you mean?"

"I left. There was no one in the house. It was on the east side, near Gastown. I got a cab and went to Charity's place. Then Matthieu brought me here."

I felt Reynold's attention change. If I didn't know Val, I would be suspicious too. I cut him off and started my own questions. I figured it would be easier coming from me. "Val, do you think they let you go?" She'd said that earlier, maybe a reminder would dig out the details.

"It crossed my mind. But the more I think about it, I'm sure they just left me there, and it would have been okay with them if I didn't get out."

Reynolds gave me a look that said I should leave the questioning to him. "Do you have the address?"

Val told him.

"Is there anything else you think I should know?"

"No." She blinked her eyes again, almost failing to get them open. "What are you going to do?"

He slipped the notebook into his pocket. "We'll investigate. You concentrate on healing."

He left, and Val watched until he was out of the room. "What are we going to do?"

I patted her hand. It wasn't helpful, but it gave me some comfort. "We'll check who owns the house. Maybe it will have a connection to the place where Angelique was killed."

She lay back against the pillows. "Okay. When I get out of here tomorrow, we can start investigating for real, right?"

I knew that feeling, too. And I knew she wouldn't have much stamina even if they let her go. "As long as the doctor gives you the okay to leave. No pretending you're well enough just to investigate."

She took a deep breath before answering, "Yeah, you're a great role model for that. I promise, though."

"How do you feel about Rory?" I asked, thinking that she needed something other than the beating in her mind as she fell asleep.

"He's not that bad. Maybe he's okay." Her words were slurred.

I pressed the button to lower the bed and helped her slide down under the blanket. "Rest and don't worry about the investigation."

I joined Matthieu and Rory in the hall. Rory looked up from his phone. "Can I go back?"

I held his arm to stop him from disturbing her. "She's resting. I'm worried about someone coming to find her. Matthieu, did Reynolds say anything about sending a guard?"

Matthieu started to answer, but Rory broke in, "No, he didn't seem to be worried about her at all. I can stay here. Let me stay."

He tried to pull away from me, but I tightened my grip. "Matthieu, you should go home. I'll stay, and then I can bring her to my place tomorrow."

Rory pulled his arm out of my grasp but stayed with us. "Dude, we can take shifts. I'll stay for a few hours. You go start investigating and come back later."

I didn't want to leave Rory here to face anyone looking for Val. I also didn't want to have to deal with his father if something went wrong. "Actually, you're right. I can be more effective if I get rest and then start looking into this house where they held her. But I've got a better idea. I know someone I can call to keep an eye on Val."

I had some connections, not all of them from the PI business. I had a buddy in the Hells Angels who owed me a favor, and would probably sit outside Val's room, or get someone to do it. "You both go home, and I'll wait until I get someone here."

Rory shook his head. "No. I'm staying. She might wake up and be scared."

"Rory, I don't want you here if someone comes after her. My

buddy is tough. He'll keep her safe." I took his arm again. "I promise. She will be safe."

"But what if she wakes up? Dude, would you like to wake up alone in the hospital?"

I'd done it a couple of times, and he was right, it wasn't a great idea. But I still wasn't going to let him stay. "She knows you care. You're going to need to be rested tomorrow. You know she's not going to sit at my place while we investigate."

"I want to stay here until this guy comes," he said.

It felt more like he'd capitulated than agreed. "Rory, we'll both stay until my friend arrives. If Val wakes up, we'll make sure he makes her feel safe."

"Right," he said before marching into Val's room.

THIRTY

I picked up Val the next morning and took her back to my place. She was in rough shape, and I'd been thinking about how we could include her in our activities without make her worse. If I could minimize her exposure, maybe I could keep her safe. "You need a disguise," I said. "I don't want anyone grabbing you again."

She looked surprised. "You aren't going to lock me in your house to keep me safe?"

"If I thought it would work, I'd do it. But I'm pretty sure you'd dig through the walls to get out. It's better if we don't let you run on your own."

She brightened as much as her swollen face would allow. "Okay. I'm pretty sure they didn't care if I left. But a disguise could be cool." She picked through the items I'd laid out on the bathroom counter. "I like this." She held up a bottle of blue hair dye.

I ignored the image of her and Rory with matching hair, like an old married couple with matching Hawaiian shirts. Reading the instructions on the bottle, I said, "Okay, you dye your hair and I'll dig out some clothes. We'll minimize the bruising with some makeup."

While Val was getting ready for our day of investigating, I did my own preparation. I called the development office to find out if Penelope was in, she was. I called Jude to see if Ink & Needles was open, no answer. And I called Rory to see if he would join us. Three sets of eyes would mean we had less chance of getting caught following our target. He didn't answer, so I left a message.

Matthieu was back in court, but he promised to do some research on Angelique when he could find wifi. I dropped a jumbo bottle of aspirin in my purse. Val was going to need painkillers, and she refused anything stronger. Then I sat on the couch to wait.

Val came downstairs wearing the hoodie and sweatpants I'd put out for her. She looked anonymous. "Great work. Will your hair survive?"

She flipped back the hood and grinned before wincing. "I decided not to dye my hair, but I used your Vaseline to make it gross so I could twist it into dreads. I guess it'll come out eventually. Or I can shave my hair."

"I'm sure we can get a hairdresser involved, and you won't have to shave. Are you ready?"

She shrugged. "I guess so. I... I don't smell."

"No." I wondered if that had to do with Rory. "You'll be fine."

"No, I mean shouldn't I stink? Like, I look like I've been on the streets for months, but I don't smell."

She had a good point. "I don't think anyone will get close enough to notice."

We arrived in New Westminster around ten am. Rory sent a text just as we exited the parkade. He was waiting for us in Starbucks, and Penelope was still in the office.

I nudged Val. "That boyfriend of yours is getting into this pretty deep."

"Rory, isn't... Yeah, I guess he is my boyfriend for now. But don't let him know that." She elbowed me and laughed without moving her face. "Look, I don't think it's such a hot idea for me to come into Starbucks. We shouldn't be seen together, right?"

Val had a point. It didn't look natural for a street kid to be hanging out with me. I didn't look like a social worker. "Do you have your phone?"

"Yeah, you guys text me with what you need. I'll be down there." She pointed at the shadows under the parking ramp.

I nodded. "Be careful." I handed her the bottle of painkillers. "You'll need these."

Starbucks was lined up when I got there, but Rory called my name and held up a cup. "Here I figured you'd need it."

I took the coffee and sipped. He'd remembered how I like it. "You'll make someone a great boyfriend someday."

He blushed, but a smile showed that he was pleased. "Yeah, tell Val that maybe."

He sounded so hopeful I almost broke Val's confidence. Instead, I brought him up to date on the plan.

"Okay, dude. So, let's get going. I have a good feeling about this plan. That chick is going to make a mistake, and we're gonna be there."

The enthusiasm of youth was contagious, and dangerous. "Don't get cocky, Rory. We need to be careful. This is going to take as much luck as skill. If she gets in a car or a taxi we're screwed."

"But we can just get a cab," he said. "I'm telling you, I have a good feeling."

I stopped his next words. "Rory, I don't want to have to tell your dad you've been hurt."

His face closed. "Yeah, see how people change when they know I'm the son of the Almighty Rance MacDonald?"

I was sure he'd been fighting his father's fame since puberty. In my experience that's when kids stop seeing their parent as heroes and start to see them as inconveniences. "It's not his fame that I'm worried about. He's your father. I don't want to have to tell anyone's father that I've let their kid get in over his head."

"Yeah, sure. I guess I kind of overreacted." His phone buzzed. "It's Val. Shit. Penelope is on the move."

I looked over my shoulder to see Penelope striding along Columbia toward the building site, a shuffling street kid trailing her by a block. "Val's got her. Let's go. I don't think she's heading to the building site. There's no entrance on this side." I would talk to Val about doing what we agreed later.

I watched from across the street as Penelope marched past the boards in front of the building facade. She didn't even glance inside to see if people were working. She kept going past the theater, paused outside Ink & Needles, and then turned toward Front Street.

Val glanced at us and sent a text. *Do you want to take over?*

I could still see Penelope, so I texted back. *Yes. You keep going and wait beside the Salvation Army store.*

Rory and I crossed the road and hurried down the side street. Penelope had reached the bottom and turned. He looked up and down the street. "Dude, what if she's gone?"

"There are only so many places she can be. We'll split up if we have to."

We didn't have to deal with splitting up. Penelope was half a block away and so focused on her destination we could have walked right behind her. This woman didn't seem to be afraid of anything. Maybe she had a reason to be that way. Maybe we should be more afraid of her.

Rory nudged me. "I think she's headed for that antique store. Remember where she got the glove."

I pulled Rory back. He'd sped up as the words came out of his mouth. It wasn't a good tailing approach to rush after your target when you thought you knew where they were going. "Hold on, Rory. We're not going to catch her doing anything in a store, except maybe shopping. We need to find a place to hang out, so we can watch her leave." I also didn't need the shopkeeper saying anything about the glove while we were there and pointing us out.

He slowed. "Sure, what do you suggest?"

There wasn't any real option that would allow us both to be standing somewhere without looking like we were following her. It would be better if there was a convenient shop to lurk in, but nothing was open.

"I think we need to split up now. I can go wait near the Sally Anne. Maybe you can pretend to check out the surplus store." There wasn't much cover at the Salvation Army donation drop off, so I figured that I'd have a better shot at making it work, because I had more experience in observing people.

He glanced around. "Okay, but can you check on Val when you go past?"

I nodded and gave him a little shove in the direction of the surplus store. He wasn't the only one worried about Val. I would get a chance to see her sitting in the plaza if I walked to the end of the street. It might be a better cover anyway. I could see the antique store from the edge of the plaza without seeming suspicious.

Val was perched on a concrete bench alone and hunched over. I hoped she wasn't as depressed as she looked. Either she was a better actor than I'd thought, or she'd learned the pose from helping the street people. I reached the stairs to the overpass and leaned against the rail to check my emails and keep an eye on the door to the antique shop.

Val noticed me after a few minutes but didn't come over. I realized that I was trying to do two things at once, and I wasn't doing either well. I kept getting distracted from watching the store by checking on Val.

It was probably more for my benefit than hers, anyway. Even though she was really just a child in age, she was probably more adult in experience than I would ever be.

I didn't have any siblings, but I knew Emma wasn't doing a great job in the role of older sister. She seemed to want to leave Val in the past with all memories of working the streets, running from gangs, and whatever else had happened to them. I just wanted to let Val be the kid she never was. Maybe it was too late, but maybe not.

My phone buzzed. *Dude, should we follow?*

I looked up to see Penelope walking toward the surplus shop. I texted a quick, *yes, be careful* and hurried to catch up. Out of the corner of my eye, I saw Val make her way toward me, her persona firmly in place.

THIRTY-ONE

I watched Penelope walk past Rory. He stayed in place but kept his eyes on the window so she wouldn't see him. Good idea, but I don't think she was aware of anything other than her goal. Wherever she was going, it was important to her.

When she was a few steps past, Rory moved away from the store and started following. I was a block away and Val was beside me.

"Are we going in the antique store?" Val asked.

I didn't want to lose Penelope, and I didn't want to leave Rory and Val alone following someone who could be dangerous. I also didn't think her visit to the store was important, at least beyond her buying a new piece of vintage accessory.

"Do you think you can get anything out of the shopkeeper?" I glanced at her. "I mean, your disguise isn't meant to reassure."

"I can deal with it." She pulled off her hood and tied her dreadlocks into a ponytail. "I'll be extra polite."

It could work. I would rather she be inside getting no information than on the street with me and in danger. "We'll text you when we have something."

She nodded and reached to open the door.

I headed down the street to where I'd seen Rory last. They couldn't be too far away, there weren't that many side streets for Penelope to take down here. After a few blocks, her choice was to turn around or maybe go into The Army & Navy store to get back up to Columbia. If she wasn't at the building site, she wouldn't be hard to find.

My phone vibrated just as I passed the surplus store. *We're on Columbia and 4th. She's moving fast.*

I hurried to catch up with Rory. It was only a block and a half, but it was uphill. You'd think all this running around New West would mean I was getting in better shape, but no.

Rory was waiting for me at the corner. "Wow, do you need an ambulance?"

"Don't be a smart ass," I managed to gasp out. I looked around as I got my breathing under control. Penelope was checking the listings outside a realty office. I guess she was doing some competitive research, except she was checking her watch, and looking at the street, more than she was reading the signs. "She's waiting for someone."

"Dude, I thought that too. It's weird she's meeting someone on the street. Or do people do that? Meet in public about crimes?"

"People do all kinds of weird things, Rory. We need to get closer to hear what's going on." I looked around. The store next to the real estate agent's was closed, a for lease sign in the window. The store on the other side was a gift shop. "You go stand in the gift shop doorway. I'll stay here until whoever she's meeting shows up. Maybe I'll get an idea when I know who it is."

"Okay, dude. I'll record what happens. What do I do if she leaves?"

"Follow her, carefully. And let Val know where we're going. I'll be right behind you."

He wandered down the street and past Penelope to stare at the bric-a-brac in the window of the gift shop. I leaned against the wall and pulled out my phone, pretending I was checking emails, while I kept an eye on our suspect.

Penelope was not happy. I didn't think she wanted to wait around. But the more I thought about it, the person she was meeting was smart. It was safer to meet her in public, no matter what they were up to together.

Val texted *the woman said P just browsed. I don't believe her. Be in the plaza.*

I didn't reply. I was watching someone walk toward the realty store. He was intent on observing Penelope who had pulled out her own phone and was jabbing at the keys. The newcomer dodged a woman with a baby in a stroller, and then stopped just short of Penelope.

I had been hoping I was wrong, but when she handed him a fat envelope, it was clear that Jude was working with Penelope.

My phone buzzed in my hand. I looked down quickly so I didn't lose track of the two conspirators.

DUDE!

I smiled, and then slid my phone into my pocket. I wanted to get closer, but there was no way I could do it without making it apparent I was listening to what they had to say. I just hoped Rory was paying attention.

Whatever Jude said to Penelope, she didn't like it. Her body tensed, and I could see her hands clench at her side. Jude was talking and leaning in close. It could have been a lover's tiff, or he could have been threatening her life. I wondered if he'd been the one who killed Angelique. Had he even been legitimately working at her shop?

The conversation ended, and Penelope marched toward Starbucks. Jude watched her go, a nasty smile crossing his lips.

Then he turned and started walking back toward Ink & Needles.

Rory stepped out of the doorway and looked at me. I had to make a quick decision. If I had been alone, I would have gone after Jude, but now we had the ability to follow two potentially dangerous people – two possible multiple murderers.

I watched Jude enter the shop and beckoned Rory over. When he joined me, I tried to keep my attention on Starbucks and Ink & Needles, and Rory at the same time. "I want you to just keep your eye on Jude. Let me know if he leaves the store."

"What about Val?"

"She's safe in the plaza right now."

He stepped back trying to see into the plaza, but it was too far. "No, dude. She won't be happy to find out we had two people to follow and we left her out."

I decided to deal with the fallout from that later. "Rory, she's hurt, and I don't want it to get worse."

"It's Val. You know her better than I do, but I don't think she's going to sit in the plaza for much longer."

I couldn't argue. I did have to stop protecting her, but not right now. "Okay, have her work with you. If Jude comes out, she can follow, but only follow. He doesn't know who she is, so it should be okay. I don't want either of you going into the store. It might tip him off that we're watching. "

"Cool. I'll text her. You be careful with that woman."

I promised, and hoped I'd made the right decision.

I walked past the open window of the Starbucks glancing inside to find Penelope pouring milk into her coffee. This was going to be trickier now that I was alone, but I'd done it before and I would have to do it again, so there was no point in worrying about it.

I waited at the stand outside the restaurant next door, pretending to read the menu, while I waited for Penelope to come out. But it didn't seem like she was just picking up a coffee for the office. I was going to have to go in if I wanted to keep an eye on her.

Glancing down to Ink & Needles, I could just make out Rory and Val lounging on the stairs that crossed the railway tracks. Good, as long as they were there, they were safe. In times like these I really valued working alone. Because, despite what Matthieu says, worrying about partners got in the way of focusing on the investigation.

I joined the back of the line at Starbucks, half listening to the weird orders and half watching my target. She'd taken the table in the back that I'd shared with Detective Reynolds. She'd also pushed away the other chairs and tables. Interesting, she was willing to be seen with whoever she was meeting, but not to be overheard.

I gave my order, a shot in the dark, and pretended to be fascinated by the merchandise as I scoped out the seating. I needed to be close enough to hear what was going on, and far enough away that it didn't look like I was following her.

I didn't get a chance for subtlety. "Are you following me?" Penelope's voice was sharp. I didn't want a fight, but I wasn't going to run away like I'm sure she wanted. I didn't think she would outright threaten me in public.

"No. Why do you think I'm following you?" Innocence dripped from my voice – I hoped.

"You keep showing up everywhere I go," she snapped.

I looked around. "It's a small town. Do you think any of these people are following you?"

"No, but they haven't been showing up everywhere I go." She pulled out her phone. "Do I have to call the cops and get you arrested?"

That was a bit of an overreaction. "It's a public space. I need to go over my notes, and this is a good place. If you don't want to be in here with me, then maybe you should leave. I promise I won't follow." I was bluffing, of course. I figured it would be too much trouble for her to redirect the person she was meeting.

She sighed. "Just stay away from me." Returning to her table, she glared at a young couple who chose to sit nearby.

I settled into one of the easy chairs a few feet away. To show she hadn't impressed me, I sat facing her table. To minimize her need to berate me, I pulled out my phone and started scrolling through a book. I hoped she thought it was my notes.

For ten minutes I watched as she took rapid sips of the coffee and alternated between glancing at the door and checking her watch. She'd been stood up. After another five minutes, Penelope made a call. I couldn't hear what she said, but her body language told me that she was leaving a message for someone who would regret not showing up.

When she ended the call, Penelope gulped the remainder of her coffee and tossed the cup into the garbage. She stalked out, stopping beside my seat to say, "Don't follow me."

I rolled my eyes.

She turned right when she exited. I waited a minute and then tossed my half-drunk coffee into the garbage before following her.

I stepped onto the street and pretended to look around before turning right. Penelope was a block away. Her anger was apparent in the way she marched along the street. She kept a straight course, forcing people to move out of her way by ignoring that they existed.

I headed after her with some caution. When I said it was a small town, I was right, but there would be little doubt I was following her if she caught me again.

I didn't have to worry. Penelope turned and entered the jeweler's. There was no chance I would coincidentally be shopping for jewelry, so I kept going. I saw her staring at the street as I walked by. I couldn't resist a fake smile and a wave as I passed.

I would be able to see her from the plaza if I wanted to pick up her trail again, but I didn't think she'd lead me anywhere useful, or at least, useful to me, now that she was suspicious. In fact, there was a big chance she'd call the thugs and lead me into a beating if I didn't step back.

THIRTY-TWO

It took a few minutes for me to join Rory and Val on the plaza stairs. My journey took me past Ink & Needles. I wished again that the windows were uncovered. It would have helped to see if Jude was busy, or alone, or even there.

I settled beside them. "Hi, guys. How are you feeling, Val."

She looked at me and I winced. Her face was even more swollen, and she had dark rings around her eyes. "I'll live. What's next?"

Rory glared at me. "She's in pain and won't let me take her home."

As he had rightly pointed out, Val was going to do whatever she wanted. I would rather she went home and rested, but, since I knew she wouldn't, I wanted to keep her close. "She'll be in pain at home, Rory. If you've never been beaten up, believe me it feels better to be doing something than sitting waiting to heal."

Val elbowed him. "See, she knows. Charity was pretty beaten up when she took down that gang."

He didn't stop glaring. "Yeah, well. I still don't want you more hurt."

I didn't have time for this spat. Part of me was happy that he cared, and that Val let him care, but the other part knew full well that she wouldn't be safe until we tracked down the killer. "I think we need to go see Jude."

"That's the guy we've been watching for, right? What's his deal?" Val's eyes seemed to brighten with the idea of action.

I wondered how much Rory had told her. "He's Angelique's... I guess he was Angelique's employee or something."

"Yeah and we saw him talking to our main suspect." Rory stood and helped Val to her feet. "You didn't meet him. We only know who he is because we went looking for Angelique. Okay, Charity, what's the plan?"

I glanced at the shop. I didn't like the idea of going in and just asking him what he was doing, but I couldn't think of any other approach. "I'm going in to ask him some questions. You stay out here. I'll leave my phone on, and you'll be able to hear everything."

"No, that's stupid," Val said. "If he is working with the Killer Ice Queen, you might be in danger."

I hated it when she had a point. "He's already seen me and Rory together, so we'll go. Will you stay here?"

"Why can't I come? I could ask for a tattoo, be a customer." I gave her the once over and she grunted. "Okay, I guess I don't look like I can afford one."

I watched as resignation crossed her face. "We'll keep you on the phone. You'll hear everything."

"Fine."

I hoped she wasn't just agreeing so she could follow us.

Rory called her phone, she answered, and then sat listening to a nonexistent caller.

I told Rory to forget that we'd seen Jude with Penelope. "Just pretend we're still investigating. I don't want him to suspect anything."

He looked at me as though I was stupid. "Dude, do you really think you need to tell me that?"

I felt my cheeks redden. "Sorry. I don't want anyone else to get hurt."

Rory grinned and patted my elbow. "No problem, mom."

I took the hint and tried to stop worrying.

Inside the shop, Jude was at the counter with a sketch pad. He looked up as soon as the door opened. "Hi."

I saw Rory slide his phone out of his pocket as I leaned against the glass top. "Hi, I guess you heard about Angelique."

"Yeah. I'm still pretty shocked. Do the cops have any suspects?"

No, but we do. I shook my head. "It's pretty early in the investigation. Did they ask you about any enemies?"

He tossed his head to move his ponytail off his shoulder. "Angelique was a bit alternative, but she had a good heart. No one had any problems with her."

I recalled Angelique saying that Penelope didn't like her. "I'm looking into it along with the other deaths. I'd appreciate any help you can give me." I felt Rory tug my jacket. When I looked at him, he flicked his gaze to the phone. I saw the screen was blank. One of them had hung up.

"I really didn't know much about her private life," Jude said, apparently oblivious to the action. "You know she was kind of a loner."

"Okay, thanks anyway." I held out a card. "If you think of anything, give me a call."

He slipped the card into his pocket. "I will. Good luck, I hope you find who did that to her."

Rory was already opening the door as I turned away. It took all of my discipline to refrain from running out and checking on Val. I guess she was the one who hung up, and I dreaded what had happened to make her do that.

On the street, Val was standing to the side of the door. She looked fine physically, or as fine as we'd left her looking. She was steaming mad.

"That's the guy."

I looked over my shoulder. "Jude?"

"Yes. He was the one who beat me up. I recognized his voice." She reached for the door.

I stepped between her and the handle. "No. He doesn't know you've identified him. Let's see what happens."

Rory led Val away from the door. "We should tell the cops."

"I know." I wanted to find out what Jude would do first. "He's not going anywhere. Maybe he will help us out if we leave him free for a while."

We went back to the plaza. It had such a lovely view of Columbia Street that it was hard to ignore the advantage. The only other option was to get more coffee, and I was already getting jittery.

"How long are we going to sit here?" Val asked. "It feels like all we do is wait for someone to do something."

"That describes most of my job." I dug in my purse and found some mints. "Here, maybe a bit of sugar will help."

Rory laughed. "My aunt says that's why movie companies have great food. It keeps the crew and cast from going crazy. That's another business that's all about waiting."

Val dropped three mints in her mouth. "So why do you want to get into it?"

"Documentaries don't get made the same way. We go in and film what's going on. Then we spend time cutting out what doesn't work." Rory tossed a mint into his mouth. "It's different."

Val and I looked at each other and exchanged a quick grin. Val's lasted longer than mine, which meant she was starting to heal. She sank onto a stone bench. "So, what's the next move?"

I hated this part of the investigation. It was the point where I knew who the criminal was, but still needed proof. I had to work hard at keeping my mind open, so I didn't miss any obvious clues that I was wrong and screw up the results. "My gut tells me that Jude will make contact with whoever he was arguing with at the house. Someone is controlling the situation. I'm hoping he won't just make a phone call. That he'll have to meet whoever it is. Then we follow and find out what happens."

Rory pointed with his chin. "You got your wish. Check it out."

Jude was walking away from us. Then he turned the corner. "Come on. We don't want lose him."

He was headed to Front Street, so we went directly there. The streets came together just past the plaza. The front of the Salvation Army store was on Columbia and the back of it on Front Street. That's what made it handy for us to follow without being too obvious.

Jude was walking toward the building site, but I wasn't sure that was his destination. There were a few small shops, some of them pretty shady, along the few blocks between us and the building site.

He stopped and checked his phone, then texted something.

I drew the others across the street and behind a pylon. It was wide enough to hide all three of us from Jude's line of sight. There weren't any pedestrians to wonder what we were doing, and the trucks driving by paid no attention.

"He's just hanging around," Val said. "Do you think he's meeting someone?"

"Duh, babe. This is a good place to do shit like that. It's got atmosphere."

I shushed them. I was unlikely that Jude could hear us, but I didn't want them getting excited and raising their voices.

Jude was still standing alone on the street. He was definitely waiting for someone. He kept glancing toward the corner and then over his shoulder. My stomach was producing more acid with every moment we waited.

"Oh, shit." Val's breath tickled my neck.

I couldn't fault her reaction. Penelope had turned the corner and was facing Jude. From the back, I could see the tension in her body. She was angry, or scared, or maybe both.

There was a quick exchange of words then Penelope reached into her purse. I braced for a gunshot, but all she brought out was another fat envelope.

"We have to go get her." Val gave me a push, but there was no strength behind it. "She's paying him for beating me up."

"Yeah, dude. Maybe she's paying him for killing people too."

I stood my ground. "No. I think that's what they were arguing about. I think he asked for more money. Or maybe she was asking him beat someone else." I couldn't think of a more benign reason for her to give him cash twice in one day. "We don't know. We need more information." I heard the intake of breath that meant they were going to argue. "No. I think it's more than that. If he was just asking for more money, she would have found someone to deal with him. I think maybe he's got some power over her."

"So, what do we do to get the proof?" Val asked, disappointed.

Good question. I would have to work out a way to make Penelope do something incriminating. It's not how I usually tie up the loose ends of an investigation, but we needed something more than just shady meetings and suspicion.

It was time to bring in the experts. "I'll let Detective Reynolds know what we've learned. He'll pick up Jude for questioning."

THIRTY-THREE

Jude's laugh carried to us in the lull between trucks passing. He left Penelope standing on the street and walked around the corner she'd appeared from. I figured he was going back to Ink & Needles. I would let Reynolds take care of him. Val's identification would be enough to get him held by the cops for a little while.

When I called Reynolds, he asked me to send Val in to make a statement. I didn't want to be distracted from following Penelope, so I put him off. "She's pretty tired. I'll bring her in later." I ended the call before he could argue.

Penelope was still standing on the corner. We needed to get out of our hiding place. A train was coming, and I didn't want to be this close to the roar of its engines. "Val, you need to go. She won't recognize you. Don't get too close." As I finished speaking, Val stepped around me, wandered across the road, and started stumbling directly toward Penelope.

Rory cursed behind me and started after her.

I took his elbow. "She's hard to manage. You'll need to learn that." I tried to let my words come out without the frustration I felt at her actions. "And it worked anyway, look."

Penelope stepped aside to avoid contact with the homeless person who reeled toward her. Val did a great job of getting Penelope moving. As Val passed, Penelope seemed to return to life. She pulled her coat close and spun on her heel to march toward the building site.

I pulled Rory across the street as soon as Penelope's attention was focused ahead of her. We caught up to Val who was leaning against the door of an abandoned store. Rory rushed to her side. "You crazy chick, what were you thinking?"

She winked at him. Her cockiness contrasting with the dullness of her skin. She needed rest no matter what happened next.

"I got her moving. Let's go." Val pushed herself away from the door, the effort making her groan. Rory took her arm, but she shook him off. "I'm okay. Let's get this done."

My heart broke at how tough she was trying to be. When this was over, we needed to make sure she wasn't left alone again. I was not going to get another little note at the end of the case. If she needed to leave, this time, she would have to say goodbye.

I held up my hand. "Okay, she can't be too far away. You wait here while I go check out the building site. If Penelope's there, I'll call you over. If not, at least you haven't wasted your energy."

I could see she was about to argue. "No, Val. You stay here with Rory. I don't want you passing out. Remember I know exactly how you feel."

She slumped against the wall. I could see the relief just under the defiance. "Fine."

I felt bad about making her wait. "Look, here's my phone, text Matthieu with the details on Jude so he can start doing some research." I unlocked the phone before I handed it over. "I have to go. If she's not at the site, we've lost her."

Val started texting, and Rory stood watching her. Did they

remember I was going to follow a murder suspect? "I'll call you over, but you need to watch me," I reminded them.

I waited for them to acknowledge what I'd said. Rory looked up and nodded. "Dude, I'll see you. Go before she moves on."

I couldn't do any more. It was time to move or give up on following Penelope. The building site was only a block away. When I passed, I saw Penelope talking to the site supervisor. Well, I say talking, it was more like tearing a strip off him. I couldn't hear what she said, but he wasn't speaking, just getting redder and redder. When I reached the other side, I turned and waved to Rory and Val. They started to walk toward me, then split up a little. I guess they realized they didn't look like a couple.

I watched as Val, then Rory, passed the site, both looking in for a second before moving on.

"Dude, I thought you said she was there," Rory said as he stepped beside me.

"She was. I saw her argue with the site supervisor."

Val leaned against the wall. "She's gone now."

We couldn't get a break. "I can't believe it."

"We should have just gone," Val said, annoyed. "We took too much time arguing over what to do."

I felt annoyance rise. "Val, it's not that simple."

"It is. She killed all those people or had them killed. She beat me. She could be planning the next murder right now."

"That would be too dangerous. She's—"

"She's nothing. She's a killer." Val's voice cracked on the last word, and she wrapped her arm around her chest.

Rory held up a hand to stop us saying anything else. "Dudes, we need to be a team."

I blew out a breath. "Okay."

"I think we need to get something to eat," Rory said. "I think it's a blood sugar thing."

Val shook off his other arm that had been draped around her shoulders. "No, what if she's..."

"Babe, you need to eat. We'll find Penelope again."

He was right. We'd been running around for hours and needed to recharge.

We decided on Vietnamese food for lunch. Fast and tasty and might keep us going until dinner. We'd put in our orders and I was pulling out my notebook to add the new information, when Detective Reynolds appeared at the table.

"Slide over." He didn't give me a choice. I slid along the bench and he sat beside me. "I'll make this short."

I thought maybe he was tired of waiting for Val to show up and give her statement about Jude. "Can't it wait until we've eaten?" I looked at Val and thought it should wait until she'd had a night's sleep too.

"Nope. You can eat your food when I've said my piece."

Val played with her cutlery.

"Dude, Val needs some rest."

Reynolds looked at Rory. "You can call me detective."

"Yes sir."

Now that they'd established the borders of their territory, I wanted this over. "Okay, what do you have to say?"

He smoothed the tablecloth. "We've had a complaint. You've been harassing Ms. Whitehall again."

Crap. I'd counted on her not wanting to bring the cops into it. She was acting like she was innocent. I knew she wasn't. Maybe she didn't do the murder, but there was something off about her. And she'd paid Jude for something other than a tattoo. "When did she talk to you?"

He looked at me. "Does it matter?"

"No, I'm just curious."

"It was before you told me about Jude St Claire. Have you run into her since?"

Technically, the answer was no. She'd slipped away so we hadn't run into her. "No."

Rory looked like he was going to say something, then Val must have jabbed him under the table because he turned to her and said, "Hey."

"Pour me some tea, please." Val slid a glance at me and pressed her lips together. I took that to mean she'd take care of Rory, and I could take care of the cop.

I wished the waiter would deliver our lunch, so we could get rid of Detective Reynolds. "What about the fact that she paid Jude money for something. Doesn't that mean you should be talking got her?"

He looked at each of us in turn. Then he said, "We will be contacting Ms. Whitehall. Do I need to report all of my activities to you?"

I'd touched a nerve. I'm not sure if it was one I wanted to keep touching. "Okay. So, we need to stay away from the woman who is the top suspect in three murders. I can't gather any more evidence that she's involved. Is that right?"

He glanced over his shoulder. I followed his gaze and saw the waiter coming with our lunch. "You can't get caught doing that. If she presses further, you'll need Rory's father to get you out of the legal bind she'll put you in." He slid out of the bench. "Enjoy your lunch." He left the restaurant without another word.

When our food was placed on the table, and the waiter had left, Val dipped her spring roll in the sauce and tried to take a bite. Her eyes tightened with the pain of opening her mouth. She put the roll down and started cutting it into morsels. "That was weird."

"It's not the first time he's done something like that." I picked at the contents of my *pho*. "I think Penelope is pressuring someone above him. He doesn't like his orders but needs his job."

"My dad might be able to find something out." Rory handed Val a stick of lip balm. "This might help, babe."

"Don't call me babe," she said automatically, taking the balm, and rubbing it gently on her lips.

"If we can't make any headway, we'll ask him." I didn't really want to involve Rance Macdonald in the investigation. He'd have certain legal boundaries that I didn't have and didn't need.

"So, what do we do next?" Val asked.

Great question. "I don't think we should go after Penelope right away. I was wondering how to find out what Penelope's connection with Jude is."

Val grunted. "She paid him to beat me up, and maybe to kill people."

"Val, I meant why would she pick him? They must have a connection from the past. You don't just go up to a stranger and ask them to do violence. Well, you don't go up to people like Jude. Thugs are different."

She nibbled at her food. "So what? We wait for Matthieu to find something?"

I had a plan, but I didn't want to involve them. "We need to split up. Val needs a shower and some rest before she gives her statement. I'd feel better if you stayed with her, Rory."

"I'm fine." Val struggled to sit up from where she was hunched over her food.

"No, you aren't. You're going to feel a lot better when you've washed your hair and had a few hours' sleep. I'm not arguing. Eat your lunch before you pass out in your plate."

THIRTY-FOUR

I got Val settled in her apartment and avoided letting them know what I was planning. I wasn't going to involve anyone, let alone the son of a lawyer, in a premeditated crime. Back on the street, I called Matthieu. "I don't have much time. Did you find anything on Jude?"

"Only a little. I am waiting for more information from some databases that perhaps I should not be touching."

I laughed. "Good to know you're not hemmed in by your previous profession."

"As you know, people change. It is not illegal. Perhaps it is presumptuous of me to use my access codes. But no one has taken away my access, so I choose to believe they want to support me in my new endeavor."

That didn't sound like the *gendarmerie* I knew. "Hah, more likely the order to remove your passwords is sitting in a big pile of other paperwork."

"This is true. I am surprised how much I have come to value bureaucracy now that I am no longer required to participate," he admitted.

The main reason Matthieu had left the *Gendarmes* was the

box they kept forcing him to work in. "Okay, what do you have on him right now?"

"I believe there is a connection between Mr. St Claire and Ms. Whitehall. So far, it is only the fact that they both lived in Toronto at the same time. They appear to have left at the same time."

I was disappointed. I didn't realize I'd been hoping so much for a break. "That's not enough for the cops. Toronto is a big city."

"Should I email you any information as it comes in? Or, perhaps, you are planning something that needs you to be undisturbed?"

How did he know? "Undisturbed would be good. My phone will be off for a while."

He made a sound of agreement. "When should we be worried that you have not turned it on?"

"A couple of hours." I hoped it would take less. "I'll call you when I'm done."

"Take care, Charity. I do not want to be the one to take bad news to Lu."

"You won't." I crossed my fingers, and then walked toward my destination while making a call to Detective Reynolds.

"Hi. I just want to let you know that Val will be in to make her statement in a few hours. I made her take a rest."

"Probably for the better. I wouldn't want her passing out in the middle of giving it."

I couldn't get a handle on this guy. Good cop bad cop wasn't generally a one-person tactic. "Where is Jude St. Claire? I want to make sure she's safe."

"He's here. He's asked for a lawyer so it will probably be a couple of hours to find one to take his case."

"Thanks."

There was a pause and then he said, "You are staying away from Penelope Whitehall, right?"

Geez did everyone know I was up to something? "Yes, I am staying as far away as I can."

"Okay, keep doing that."

I promised and ended the call. At least, neither of them had said that I should stay away from Ink & Needles. My gut said that there was something in there that could incriminate one, or both, of our suspects. I wasn't going to wait any longer. No more dead bodies or beaten girls, we needed to end this case today.

I counted on the fact that people wouldn't be paying attention if I was fast. I'd noticed the lock on the shop was old, and I was pretty sure I could pick it fast enough to look like I had a key. Once Jude was actually under arrest for battery, there was a good chance that the cops would seal the shop. This might be my best opportunity to snoop.

I was grateful this time for the fact that the windows weren't clear. The small recess from the street to the door was much more private because of it.

My picks were in my hand when I stepped up to the door. I slid the wrench into the keyhole and then the pick. The tumblers fell into place, and I was inside the shop within seconds. As I shut the door behind me, I suddenly thought about an alarm, but nothing beeped or flashed. No security system, just the cowbell. I'd lucked out. I turned the latch, so I wouldn't be disturbed.

It was dark in the lobby. I couldn't remember seeing a light switch when I was here before. Picking locks was probably the easiest part of a burglar's job. I needed to get into the habit of casing rooms just on the chance I might need to break in.

I pulled on a pair of gloves, took my pocket flashlight from my purse, and began my search. The display case had sheets of drawings and photos of tattoos. They looked pretty standard.

No secret file, no incriminating evidence. The cash register was open and empty.

The shop consisted of the front lobby, a back room with two reclining chairs and a lot of ink, and equipment that might have fit well into a torture dungeon. Beyond that was a washroom, small closet, and a wall. No back door, no office.

A quick glance around the washroom and closet showed me only functional spaces. No secret wall safe, or anything.

The tattooing room was going to take a while. As I shone my flashlight around, I noticed that it wasn't just a common space. Angelique had the chair on the right and Jude the chair on the left. On Angelique's side, everything was neat, and the counter was clear. The clue that it was her space was the cardigan on the chair and a picture of her with a young boy. What I hadn't expected was a bill for rental of the nightclub basement. That's why she'd never denied being a member of the sex club, she ran it.

On Jude's side, it wasn't exactly messy, but there were ink pots open and the counter held a man's watch and a leather jacket.

I started going through Jude's side of the room. Two minutes later I had an envelope in my hand. There were two items inside, a DNA test result, and a photo of a dead body.

I put them on the counter, took a few pictures with my camera, and carefully returned the items to the envelope. Then I put the envelope back in its hiding place. All that was left to do was find a way to get the cops to search the place so they could find this. Time to split.

As I passed through the curtain to the lobby, I heard the door rattle. I froze. Was Jude free?

"Hey, come on, man," a rough voice called. "We had a deal."

I considered waiting him out, but I didn't want to spend any more time than necessary in here. And he was still rattling the door despite the fact that no one had answered, so I figured he wasn't going away.

Moving to stand next to the door, I deepened my voice. "Who are you looking for?"

"Who is that?"

"You don't need to know that. What do you want?"

"Jude. He was going to finish my tat today." He slammed his fist against the doorframe. The cowbell clanked, but the door held.

"Yeah, he got delayed. He'll be back in an hour."

"You sure?"

"Yeah, he's gone for supplies." I held my breath praying that he would believe me.

His hand smacked into the door frame again. "Damn. Fine, I'll be back in an hour. You'd better be open then."

"We will be."

I let go my breath. I could hear him swearing, then, with a kick to the door frame, he continued to share his limited vocabulary with the world, but his voice faded. The lock might be old, but the door was solid. I counted to fifty then let myself out. The lock was one you could set on the inside, so I just had to shut the door behind me.

THIRTY-FIVE

I called Matthieu to confirm I was still alive and went back to Val's place. The door was unlocked. Rory was in her living area, drinking tea and making notes on his phone.

He looked up as I closed the door behind me. "Dude, what the heck, you look like you are about to have a stroke."

I flopped into one of the easy chairs in Val's living room. There were two chairs, a love seat, a coffee table, and not much else. "I had a scare. But I've got some information we can use. You should have locked the door."

"Yeah. I figured it would be better if you didn't have to knock and disturb Val." He put his phone down. "Can I see the information?"

"It's still where I found it. I didn't exactly ask for permission to go hunting around the tattoo shop."

His eyes widened. "You broke in? Cool."

I gave him the short version of the story. "Now we need to figure out how to get the evidence in the hands of the police."

He got up. "Tea? A bit of caffeine will probably help."

"Yes, please. Has Val been asleep long?" The kitchen was

open to the living room. We could keep a conversation going without making too much noise.

Rory checked his watch. "Yeah, she went to sleep right after you left. Dude, I don't want to wake her, she is in pretty bad shape."

"No, we don't need her for this. Val needs a couple of hours' sleep, and then she'll have to make that statement."

Rory made me some herbal tea. So much for the caffeine. I showed him the pictures I took, and then sent them to Matthieu.

Rory stared at the picture. "Dude, how does this help? I mean it's a dead body."

I enlarged the image and moved it around until he could see the details. "Look. The newspaper. I think whoever took this picture put it there to make the link. It's an issue of the Toronto Sun. That's the day the cops found that body at Penelope's listing."

He squinted at the details. "You think maybe Jude did the murder and is holding something else? Something that makes it look like this Penelope did it, or hired him to do it?"

"I hope so. I think the DNA test is the link. My guess is that he has a story linking the picture and the DNA test to prove who really killed the man."

"Maybe the test is her blood, or maybe it's two tests, or... Man, this would make a great documentary."

He was right, it would have been a great on-line documentary, and it could have given him the break he needed. That sort of thing happened all the time these days. Someone puts their talent on YouTube, and they become celebrities. "I'm sorry, Rory, but I'm not sure how you would have filmed that without identifying me. And I think your dad would have a problem if there was video of you committing breaking and entering."

"Yeah, I guess you're right." He didn't sound too broken up.

I tried not to let that bother me or think about why he was

unconcerned. "You know, when this is over, maybe Jake can get you an introduction to someone who can help you." It wouldn't hurt to ask, and Jake knew a lot of people in the industry.

"Really? That would be cool. Thanks, Charity."

I'd graduated from dude to my name. I wasn't sure if that was a compliment.

"Maybe I can help with an idea." Rory started packing his backpack with scattered equipment and notes. "My dad, I could ask him how to get some evidence to the cops. So they can use it."

Rance MacDonald would probably have kittens at the thought of introducing evidence, given the way I'd found the photo and test results. My doubt must have been all over my face because he added, "Dude, I won't give him the details. He'll be cool. I'll say it's for a documentary. I promise he won't know you did anything illegal."

He stood there waiting for my permission to help. "Okay. It would be useful to know the possibilities. Just be careful. As a lawyer, he has an obligation to report things like this."

Rory rolled his eyes. "Dude, I've had that lecture a million times." He packed up the last of his items. "I'll probably have to wait for him to come out of court, but don't worry, I'll get you some info."

I followed him to the door and made sure it was securely locked behind him. Val was still sleeping, and I needed to think. I settled in the chair and started tossing ideas around in my head.

THE NEXT THING I KNEW, I was woken by the sound of someone washing dishes. Val was up and in the kitchen. I checked the time on my phone; two hours. I'd slept for two hours. It was late and I wanted desperately to get this case finished today. I was just tired of running around and only getting a step closer, if that. It felt like I was waiting to live my life after Penelope got arrested. I usually didn't stick with one case all day and night, so maybe this was normal.

Val stood behind the love seat drying her hands on a tea towel. "I guess we have to go make my statement now."

I nodded. "It probably won't be a full statement. I think you'll just need to add some information to the statement you already made."

She looked around. "I guess Rory had something to do."

I hid my smile. "He's gone to talk to his dad about something."

"Oh," she said.

"You like him, right?" I wanted to know if I should be helping, or hindering, a romance. "You know he likes you."

"Are we in high school?" She laughed to soften the words.

I wished she'd just be straight with me on this. "Nope, I think it's more serious than that. What about your last boyfriend?"

She started tidying the cushions. "I haven't ever had a boyfriend."

"Oh. I figured you'd have had relationships in the last year or so."

She picked up the throw that I'd been wrapped in and started to fold it. "I've been busy. And I didn't really know how to have a relationship instead of... you know."

I guess making the transition from teenage prostitute to girlfriend would be difficult. "I'm no expert. I don't think anyone really is. But I think Rory is a nice guy. You should give him a chance."

She shrugged. "I guess so. When do I tell him about my past?"

I had no idea. "Maybe not until you know him a bit better. But don't wait too long."

"We'll see." She tied her hair into a ponytail. It accented the bruises on her face, but it was a definite improvement on the fake dreadlocks. "What is Rory checking with his dad?"

I told her about the evidence.

"So, you are still willing to break into a building to get what you need. At least this wasn't some warehouse in the East end." She sat. "I have an idea."

"Okay, shoot." Whatever she said it was better than the nothing I had. Sleeping when I was supposed to be planning wasn't useful.

"I'm going to give a statement about Jude, right. How I know he was one of the people who kept me in that house and beat me." She pointed to her face. "What if I remember something he said? Something that gets them to search Ink & Needles?"

It was tempting. "I don't know if it will work, if you lie to them. That's what Rory is asking his dad, for some ideas that we can use."

"What if I didn't lie? What if I... I don't know... hinted. Like, what do you think I should say?"

"Val, I think it's —" I stopped talking. She was right. We didn't have a plan. Whatever Rance MacDonald said, he wasn't going to endorse my actions. "Maybe the fact that Angelique is dead, and Jude worked in the tattoo place, will be enough to get a warrant to search it."

"And maybe they won't make the connection," Val said.

I wanted to say that the cops would make the connection, but I didn't really have a lot of confidence in that statement. Detective Reynolds may be cooperating, but I still didn't feel like he had the same incentive as we did to solve the case.

"Come on, Charity, just a little push." The look on her face said I couldn't stop her anyway.

"Okay, we need to have something to link the tattoo place with a crime. It has to be something different from your beating because they already have him on that."

"What about Angelique's murder. I could say I heard him arguing about that with the mystery woman." She made air quotes with the statement. "If he denies it, I could say later that I was confused because of the pain."

I tried to think of a good argument against her plan. I couldn't. The fact that she was in pain could make the retraction valid. "Before we go any further with it, let me see if Rory has talked to Rance," I said.

Rory didn't answer his phone.

Val jumped up and grabbed a sweater. "Let's just do it. How come you get to break into places, and I can't help by telling a white lie."

I told myself there was a difference, it was infinitesimal, but it was different. "It's not a white lie, it's a lie. It could mean they get away with murder because the police can't use evidence they find."

She glared at me. "And if they find out you broke into the store?"

I gave up. "Okay, just be careful. I don't want you in trouble."

She rolled her eyes. "I won't be. Come on."

I admired her confidence. "Just be careful."

"Yes, mom."

I wasn't sure I liked being called that twice. My phone rang before we made it out the door. I looked at call display. "It's Penelope."

THIRTY-SIX

I held the phone out so Val could hear the whole conversation. "Why are you calling?" I was in no mood to be nice. She couldn't get the police to warn me one second, and call me the next, and expect me to treat her like a friend.

"We should meet." She was apparently in the same mood.

"Why?"

"I think you need to hear my side of the events. I think maybe we started out on a misunderstanding." She kept her voice flat. I figured she didn't want to antagonize me unnecessarily. "I know why these people were killed."

I looked at Val. She nodded and mouthed *now*. She could make her statement later. How long could it take to meet Penelope and hear her out? I hoped she would let something slip. That way we could take something more to Detective Reynolds. We could even record her. "Okay. Let's meet right now. Where are you?"

"I'm at one of my listings." She gave me an address that was only a few blocks from the house where we found Angelique.

"On my way." I ended the call. "Okay, Val, you go give your statement and I'll meet her."

"No way. You are not going to meet her alone. She's dangerous."

I guess I should have expected the argument. "I don't like it either, but you are in no shape to come with me."

"No. I'm not leaving you to go there alone. I don't want to hear you are the next body." Her voice cracked. "Get Matthieu to go with you."

Going alone was probably a bad idea, but as long as someone knew where I was, I couldn't get in too much trouble. "He'll be at home. We don't have time to wait for him. I'll be okay." I know that sounded more confident than I really felt. "Look, I'll call Matthieu, but I can't wait for him."

She grabbed a jacket. "At least let me sit in the car. I won't be able to think straight to give my real statement, let alone come up with a way to get the cops to search Ink & Needles."

I told myself that the car would be safe. She could lock the doors, and she would be safe. "Okay. You have to promise to stay in the car. I will try to keep you on the phone. You hang up and call the cops if there's anything fishy." I waited until she promised, and then called Matthieu.

"Charity, you must wait for me to arrive."

Everyone seemed to think this could wait. This was the first real opportunity I had to get Penelope to incriminate herself. "No. She might change her mind. What if she's in the confessing mood?" I motioned for Val to open the door. This conversation would need to be done on the move.

"Yes, and it is more likely she is in the killing mood." I heard Lu asking what was going on. "I must go out and stop Charity getting herself killed."

Lu's voice came through clearly. "Charity, stop being an idiot."

"I don't want to do this, but it might be our only chance."

"Wait for Matthieu, or better yet, call the cops in."

Val and I were at the car. "Val will be in my car outside the house. How long will it take you to get here, Matthieu?"

"I am leaving now. A half hour?" Matthieu made some comment to Lu that I couldn't make out. "Charity, I understand why you don't want to call the police right now. And I know you are able to handle yourself on most cases. This one is not most cases."

"I know," I said. "I have to go, Matthieu. I'll text you the address. Put it in your GPS and meet us there."

I heard a door slam in the background. "Be careful. I do not like this."

"I know. Okay see you at the house."

We made it to the address in ten minutes. We found a good parking spot in another five. Val would be able to see the front of the house while I was inside. We checked the battery level on our phones, something we should have thought of before leaving. I blamed it on having to argue with Matthieu.

Val's phone was half dead. "It should be good until Matthieu gets here," she said.

I held her chin to make her meet my eyes. "Whatever happens, you don't come in."

She looked right at me. "Sure."

I didn't believe her. "Val, I need to know you'll be safe."

"Yeah, I need to know you'll be safe, but I have to settle for this." She held up her phone.

"I'm sorry." I was really sorry that she was there, and that I had to leave her. "When Matthieu gets here, you can decide what to do. Just leave your phone on mute."

"Okay."

I left the car and locked the doors.

The street was empty. Most of the houses were dark, or well closed up with only a little light leaking from around the curtains.

THIRTY-SEVEN

The front door was ajar. I pushed it fully open and waited. No one stepped out, no one shot at me. The house might as well be deserted. Stepping inside to the foyer, I smelled old house, stale air, mildew, and mouse. From the outside, it looked like a slightly run-down heritage style house. From the inside, it seemed to be about to crumble around me.

"I'm here," I called. "Penelope?"

"In the back."

I didn't want to go any deeper into the house. I didn't know what the back was like. Here, I could run if I needed. The front door was only steps away, and it was wide open. "I'll wait here."

"Nope, come to me. I need to stay with what I'm doing." There was no opening for argument in her tone. The implication was come to me, or you don't get the information.

I went. I dug into my pocket for my car keys, the only thing I could turn into a weapon. I told myself I wouldn't need it. That she wouldn't try anything. I even tried to convince myself that I was wrong, and she wasn't the killer. None of it worked, but I kept walking.

I passed through a hallway and into the kitchen. Penelope

was there with a set of plans laid out on the cracked tile counter-top. She looked up as I entered. "Great. What do you think of this place?"

She was crazy. No indication that she might be a killer, no reference to her obstructive actions. "I didn't come here to discuss real estate."

"I know, but I'm interested in your opinion. Besides, I hate just jumping in to business." She stood back and waved an arm around the room. "What do you think?"

The kitchen was in worse shape than the front of the house. "Aren't you just going to pull it down and put a handful of townhouses?"

She glanced at the plans. "If I can, but New West is kind of picky about its heritage. I'm waiting for approval of my plans."

"The politician? You were trying to get an edge?" Or a bribe? Or blackmail?

She smiled. "Yes, but he wasn't interested. Some people are too honest for their own good."

I didn't really care. Politicians and developers were old buddies in the Vancouver market. "Can we get down to it?"

She rolled the plans and put them in a cardboard tube. "Show me your phone first."

How did she know? "Why?"

She held out her hand. "I'm going to tell you some things I'd rather not get recorded."

I pulled it out of my pocket, hanging up on Val as I did. "See, it's off."

"Good." She looked over my shoulder. "That didn't take long."

I spun to see who she was talking to.

Val was there with one of the thugs holding her by the arm. "Nope, she was right outside."

I didn't say anything. I'd save it for when we got out of this mess. When Matthieu arrived, he'd find my car empty. I knew he'd call the police when that happened. It was only a matter of ten or fifteen minutes. I could keep them talking that long.

"So, what's going to happen?" That topic wouldn't hold them for more than a few seconds, but I struggled to think of what else to say.

"Yeah, are you going to kill us? Isn't the body count getting too high?" Val's words were punctuated with a cry of pain as her captor twisted her arm behind her back.

Penelope opened her purse and drew out a gun. "Gag them both and throw them in the van. We'll deal with this at the house."

"You can't kill both of us with the one gun. No matter how many bullets you have, it only shoots one at a time," I said.

"I'm fast on the trigger," Penelope answered in a reasonable tone. "But the kid won't put up a fight. Look at her; she's almost falling over right now. So, I just shoot you first then her."

Val glared at her, but Penelope was right. She didn't have to kill both of us. I had to find a way to leave Matthieu a clue. Otherwise we were in major trouble. The problem is I didn't have anything to drop that would point to our destination. Even if I did, I had no idea what the destination was.

Stalling was my only real option. "Won't people see you escorting us out?"

We watched the thug put tape over Val's mouth and Ziptie her hands together. Then he handed her to Penelope and came toward me with a strip of duct tape for my mouth. "Go ahead, struggle. I don't mind." His eyes gleamed.

I glanced over at Penelope. She laughed. "Oh, don't worry. It doesn't hurt when it comes off, even if you are alive. And no one will see us go out the back."

I looked at the gun, and for a second, thought of rushing her. Then the thug slapped the tape over my mouth and spun me around to tie my hands. We were going to have to play along until I could get us out of this mess.

When we were tied up, the thug shoved us toward the back door. There was no garden, just a concrete pad with a white van parked facing the alley. Before I could do anything, we were tossed into the back and feeling the jolts as Penelope drove away.

THIRTY-EIGHT

When the van stopped, we were inside a garage. I heard Penelope tell the thug to put us in the basement. The back of the van opened. Rough hands grabbed the Ziptie around my wrist, dragging me from the van. He held me against the back door with one hip while reaching for Val. She groaned as he pulled her to stand beside me.

The urge to kick him in the groin and run battled with the knowledge that Val would probably not have the strength to follow me. We had to comply, at least until I could form a better plan.

I met Val's eyes, and she glanced at her pocket. I looked but couldn't figure out what she was trying to tell me. Before I could react, the thug shoved us toward a small door in the back of the garage. We were shoved into the darkened room.

I squeezed my eyes shut and counted to twenty. When I opened them again, I could see outlines of things, and shadows by the sliver of light coming under the door.

Val was standing to my right. There was a chair a few feet away, and a chain that would turn on the light to my left. I had no way of grabbing the chain. I needed to get my hands free, or my mouth. If I could get Val to understand, I had a way to get the tape off my mouth.

Her eyes had adjusted, and she was still trying to tell me something about her pocket. I shook my head and moved to stand directly in front of her.

I bent my knees and looked at her. She looked at the ground, concrete and stained with something. She shrugged and knelt. I turned my back to her and reached toward her face. I felt her jerk back, and I figured that she was trying to avoid being hurt more than she already was. Then I heard a muffled grunt before I felt her face in my hands.

I knew this was going to hurt her, but there was no way to avoid it. I felt for the edge of the tape and used my nails to lift the edge. I tried to be gentle, but as soon as I had a good grip, Val jerked her head to free herself.

"Your turn," she said, standing.

I knelt, and she repeated my actions. As much as I didn't want to, I jerked to rip the tape off. It hurt as much as I expected, and then the pain was gone. "What is in your pocket?"

"My phone. They didn't take my phone."

I tried to reach into her pocket to get it, but there was no way. "Can you get it out?" I walked to the chain and pulled it with my teeth. The light bulb in the center of the room flickered on and gave a feeble forty-watt glow. It was enough to see our immediate surroundings, an empty room with two iron posts holding the weight of the house off us.

"I don't think so," she said. Then, looking around, she continued, "This looks like where they kept me before."

"Should we yell? Maybe someone will hear us?"

She went to the door and tried to open it. "No, I did a bunch of yelling before. No one came."

The door opened. Penelope stood there holding a bag. "Save

your voices. There's no one around. I own the houses on each side."

She held out the bag. I could smell hamburgers. My stomach growled.

She laughed. "If I undo the Zipties you can eat. If you promise to behave, then I will."

"We promise." I glanced at Val, hoping she would take the hint. We were better off untied. Promises made under duress weren't expected to be kept. "Where's the thug?"

"Rick? I told him to wait upstairs. I wanted to deal with you myself." She held out a pair of scissors. As much as I hated the idea of letting her close to me with them, I turned and held out my hands. She snipped the plastic and pushed me away. "You can feed her," she said waving the scissors in Val's direction.

I opened the bag and unwrapped a burger. Holding it out so Val could take a bite. I reached in to get one of the bottles, they were juice, and the bottles were glass. "Are you that confident we won't hurt you? There are two of us."

"I have this." She held up the gun. "I've always wanted to know what it feels like to kill someone."

"So, you usually hire people?" I unscrewed the cap of the juice bottle and took a sip. "How many times have you done that?"

Penelope laughed again. It was disturbing how much she was enjoying this. "I'm not going to give you all the details of my past. This isn't some TV mystery where the villain has to recap their motive and procedures."

Val had finished her meal. I held the bottle out, but she shook her head no. Placing the bottle on the chair, I unwrapped the other burger and devoured it. The second bottle of juice was sweating condensation into the bag.

"So, how are you going to do it?" Val asked. "Kill us, I mean?"

She smirked. "I don't want to rush it. But don't worry, I won't drag it out too long. I think I should just shoot you in the head, Val. You'll die nice and fast." She turned to me. "You, I don't like. I hear a gut shot is painful and slow to kill."

I moved to stand between Penelope and Val. "You know gunshots might get heard."

She reached into her jacket pocket and pulled out a metal cylinder. "I thought of that. Silencer." She screwed it on.

Val moved from behind me. "I don't think it's that easy to kill someone," she said.

I stepped between them again, glaring at Val to stay behind me. She glared back and moved to the side.

"I hear that too," Penelope said. "But you never know until you try."

By trying to protect Val, I had moved away from the chair and my only weapons. I shrugged and moved back. Reaching for the opened bottle, I took a sip and grabbed the other one. "Why?"

Penelope motioned for Val to stand against the wall. "Why what?"

"Why did you have those people killed?" I braced myself. Was she planning on shooting right now?

She raised an eyebrow. "Are you hoping to stall me until the cavalry arrives?"

"No, but if we have to die, I'd like to know."

"Yeah, why don't you tell us? Is it because you didn't have them killed? Is someone else giving the orders?" Val didn't move, but I saw the subtle shift in her stance. She was ready to run if needed.

Penelope narrowed her eyes. "Why don't you believe I ordered the killings?" Val had definitely hit a nerve.

"Well," I said. "It's not like you are some big criminal mastermind." If she was trying to prove something, it might just be the distraction we needed. "It makes sense that someone else is in charge. You don't strike me as the type to command any loyalty. In my experience, there are two things that criminal masterminds use to things done, loyalty and fear."

Her fingers tightened on the gun. I tried not to tense. I had to be ready to run, or dodge, or whatever it took to protect Val.

"I use leverage. I pay well, and I make sure I have something to use to ensure people keep their mouths shut."

She really believed that was how she kept people in control. "Is that what happened with Jude? Did he have some leverage against you? Something to make the price go up?"

"That little shit thought he did. If the cops hadn't taken him in, I would have already made my first kill. Now he's going to be my third."

I wondered how long Rick was going to stay upstairs waiting. "So, what's the end game? What are you trying to accomplish?"

I saw that we had her. She desperately needed to brag about what she was doing. "Fine. I guess it won't hurt to tell you. I needed this development to go smoothly. There are investors who don't like waiting for a return. Schell was making noises that he could block me, Ken was too nosy, Angelique found out what Jude had done for me in Toronto." It was so matter of fact that I wanted to kick her. Didn't she care about anyone? Was she so desperate to pay back her investors that she'd keep killing anyone who got in her way?

"It seems to me you are just digging a bigger hole with every death." I settled my weight and relaxed my shoulders.

"Well you, her, and Jude should be just what I need to fill the hole." She used the gun to point as she said our names, then stopped with the gun pointed at Val.

Val bent forward and charged. I threw the bottle at Penelope's arm, connecting just as Val rammed her.

The gun went off.

I lobbed the second bottle at Penelope's head, hitting her hard. She connected with the post and she went down, her head bouncing against the concrete floor.

Val staggered to a stop and turned toward me. "Charity?" Her voice seemed to be coming from a long way off. "How bad is it?"

I wondered what she was talking about for a second, then the pain roared through me. I looked where her gaze was fixed. Blood was soaking my sleeve.

"Don't pass out!" Val nudged me, and I folded. The chair caught me before I hit the ground. It was very cold in the room.

"Cut me free." Val kicked the scissors toward me. "Don't pass out and leave me tied up. I can't help if I'm tied up. Charity!" She was screaming at me; it was like she was doing it from another room.

The light bulb was dimming, or maybe that was just me. I gritted my teeth to bring my focus back. I saw the scissors and closed off everything else. Slowly reaching for them, trying not to fall over, I wrapped my left hand around the handle.

"Can you open them up? Maybe I can use them like a knife?"

This was going to be impossible. I wasn't left-handed, neither were the scissors, but I knew I was too close to passing out to try anything else. I put the scissors on my knee and opened the blades.

THIRTY-NINE

The door banged open and I heard a lot of voices. I couldn't make out any words. I kept my focus on getting the scissors open. "Val." I meant it to be a shout, but I knew it was barely a whisper.

"Charity, it's okay." It wasn't Val's voice. "Charity, it is Matthieu. It is okay, the police are here." I felt his hands on my right arm. "Thank God, it is a flesh wound. You will be fine."

"It hurts." I couldn't tell if the sound made it out of my mind.

He wrapped something around my arm. "Yes, it hurts more than a fatal shot. It is because you will live."

I was getting cold again. "Val?"

He put pressure on my arm, and the pain almost sent me into blackness, but I held on.

"She is fine. Rory has taken her outside. You saved her," he assured me.

"Penelope?"

"Hush, don't worry she will not be able to hurt you now."

I stopped fighting the blackness. The last sound I heard before I passed out was the wail of sirens.

. . .

WHEN I OPENED MY EYES, I saw a metal bar. Then I smelled the antiseptic and sour odor of hospital. My arm was wrapped in a thick bandage and was comfortably numb. There was a crowd around the bed.

"Hey, welcome back." Jake leaned over and kissed my forehead.

I tried to sit up but didn't have the energy. Then the head of the bed rose. I looked over and Val was pushing the remote control, a grin pulling the bruises and cuts on her face.

"Here," Lu said passing me a plastic cup of water. "Don't ever do anything that stupid again."

I concentrated on sipping the water. I couldn't argue with her, but sometimes stupid is the only option. After a few minutes with no one else weighing in, I figured it was safe to ask some questions. "How did you find us?"

Matthieu answered, "It was all due to Rory. When I arrived at the address you sent me, I found your car empty, and the house the same."

Val squeezed Rory's arm. "Matthieu called Rory, just in case we'd checked in with him."

Looking like the world was his to hold, Rory filled in the rest. "I found you by GPSing Val's phone. I'd installed an app so we could keep into touch. We called the cops and then came looking."

I had never been so happy about technology before. Screw the big brother aspect, Rory had saved our lives. "What happened to Penelope?"

Lu perched on the end of my bed. "What do you remember?"

"She fell. No, Val and I knocked her over. She shot me just

before." I kept my eyes on Lu. This wasn't going to be good news.

"She died." Lu knew better than to hint around. I needed bad news and good news the same way – quick and easy.

"I killed her?" I was having a hard time feeling anything. "It was an accident. I only meant to stop her shooting Val."

"Val told the police what happened. They aren't pressing charges. It was self-defense," Lu said. "Rory's dad showed up just after you passed out. He's an interesting man."

Jake put his hand on my bandaged arm. "The hospital is going to set you up with a counselor."

"For what?"

He looked puzzled. "Killing someone is a big deal."

He was right, but I still didn't feel anything. I'd been there when people died in past cases, but I'd never killed anyone. "What kind of painkillers are they using on me?"

He kissed my forehead. "Strong ones. Promise me you'll see the counselor?"

"I will." I was starting to feel the weight of my injuries, it was like a blanket of deadening wool. "When do you think I can go home?"

"Not until tomorrow at the earliest." Jake started to shoo everyone out. "Rest. We'll be back tomorrow." He looked at Val. "All of us."

"Yeah, yeah. I'm not going anywhere."

Rory put his arm around her. "Good to hear, babe."

This time she just rolled her eyes and didn't tell him to stop calling her babe.

FORTY

The hospital released me the next morning. I had a prescription for more painkillers that I was going to delay filling and hope I didn't have to. I knew too many stories of people who ended up dependent on prescription drugs, and that became the first step on the road to theft, prostitution, and other bad consequences.

Jake had picked me up and checked to make sure I had an appointment with the counselor. I'd made one first thing. I knew Jake was worried, but he didn't really know what it felt like to end a life.

Matthieu had dropped by on his way to another case. He had killed someone, so he knew what I might be feeling. "There is no shame in getting help, Charity. You are a good person. There are always consequences for good people when it comes to killing."

I was already starting to feel the consequences. I'd been woken by the memory of throwing that second bottle. I kept seeing her head hit the ground and bounce. But in my mind, her head cracked open, spilling blood and brains all over us.

I was installed on the couch in Jake's place. I couldn't

complain. He could cook and was willing to entertain my visitors. At least until he had to go back on set in a couple of days. He was in the kitchen putting some snacks on a plate while we waited for Val. "Are you going to talk about your relationship with her?"

That was Jake. He liked to talk about relationships. I just liked to have them. "What talk do you mean?"

He put the platter on the coffee table. "Look, you treat her like she's your little sister. She's not, and she's been taking good care of herself for over a year. If you don't hash out the boundaries of your relationship, it's going to blow up when she gets tired of being treated like a kid."

The gate buzzer went off before I could answer. He let her in through the security gate and I had about thirty seconds before she arrived. I dreaded the talk. What if she told me she wasn't interested in being my friend?

"Hey, Charity, are you feeling any better?" She carried a box of chocolates with her. "Chocolate can cure anything, right?"

I patted the sofa. "Yes, and yes. I'm feeling better without all the drugs, and chocolate cures everything."

Jake threw a leather jacket on and gave me a meaningful look. "I'll be right back. I forgot something at the store."

I let him go. He was giving us room to talk, so I started the subject of relationships. "How's Rory. He looked pretty upset last night."

"He's kind of hovering, but it feels nice." She picked a cracker off the platter. "I might like having a boyfriend."

"Yeah, having people in your life is nice." I sipped at my water glass. "I don't have much of a family. Lu is kind of like my sister."

"Yeah, you and me, we only have one relative each. Your

uncle Mike is hardly ever around. Emma's kind of abandoned me." She didn't meet my eyes as she spoke.

"Family is what you make it," I said. "Look at the family I've made."

"Well, I'm not ready to call Rory family." She started to unwrap the chocolates.

I let that go because this wasn't supposed to be about their relationship. "Will you stick around?"

She looked up. "Uh, yeah. I wanted to say I was really sorry about leaving you that note. Emma wanted to get away, and I had to make sure she was safe."

I nodded. "I know."

Tears were gathering at the corners of her eyes. I could feel my own responding. I blamed it on the residual drugs in my system.

Val shrugged, but I could see pain in her eyes. "She's my sister, but I think you took better care of me than she did. If Emma wasn't my sister, I'd think she was kind of a bitch. Nothing good happened to me when she was in charge."

I wanted to put my arm around her but knew she wouldn't appreciate it. "Emma was just a kid."

"Yeah, I know. But I was too." She rubbed at her eyes.

I wiped the tears from my cheeks. "You managed."

"I learned to do things. You were the one who gave me the idea to run my own business. You were the one who almost died looking after me."

"Can you let that go? Can you forgive Emma?" It would eat away at her if she couldn't.

She wiped her own tears. "Not good with compliments, huh?" She smiled. "Rory said I should talk to you about it."

I laughed. "It looks like we've both been stuck with boyfriends who like to talk about feelings."

"Let's hope they grow out of it," she said with a laugh. The tears had receded.

"Okay, here's the deal," I said. "I don't want to treat you like a kid, but I think you are more like a friend."

She laughed, this time it wasn't covering tears. "I like the friend thing. Now can we eat some chocolate and stop being such girls?"

WANT MORE?

Charity reluctantly takes a missing dog case as a favor and stumbles into an industrial espionage case that might end her life.

Use the QR code to grab a copy of AVARICE today.

Sneak peek on the next page.

If you enjoyed reading Ambition, please consider helping other readers to find the story by leaving a review.

CHAPTER 1

My name is Charity Deacon and I'm a PI at my own agency — or half agency since I'd made Matthieu my partner. These days, my life flowed from boring to dangerous. It was better than before, when it just flowed from day-to-day. I became a private investigator when I got caught up in a case a few years ago. I'd seen something at an accident that the cops hadn't. Then, somehow Val Wei had come knocking at my door the same day begging me to help find her missing sister. One minute I didn't know any teenage prostitutes the next, I had one following me around to make sure I paid attention to her case.

Before I knew it, I was deep in the world of gangs and people traffickers. I guess I'm lucky that my... boyfriend, I hate that word, doesn't try to stop me from getting in too deep.

Now, here I was sitting at my kitchen table looking at a caseload of files and feeling pretty professional.

Business was slow. It was a perfect time for Matthieu and Lu to plan their wedding. So, he'd taken a few days off. I wasn't worried; I could manage the outstanding cases. I loved calling it that. PI's took cases, not just jobs. And I had a bit of capacity to take on another small one if I wanted to.

Or, I could just enjoy the break. It's not like I hate the private investigation business; it's a great gig for a woman with a pushy personality. I just like taking breaks as much as making money. The problem right now was Jake, that boyfriend I mentioned. His acting career was taking off, but it always took him away, and because of the current cases, I couldn't hop a plane to Australia and join him.

I stacked the six current files on the dining table and decided to get productive; sitting around was just making me antsy. The first file was an embezzlement case. If I'm going to be professional, I guess it's an alleged embezzlement. A page into the file and Matthieu's notes changed my mind; hidden assets, and an expensive girlfriend — the target was guilty. All that I had to do was write up the report and send it with the final invoice.

The next two files, both Matthieu's, were on hold until the clients contacted us to do the background checks. We did a fair amount of those for private colleges and hospitals. That left three of my own files. None of them were as organized as Matthieu's, but I knew exactly what was going on.

The warehouse: a few too many items falling off the back of a truck. I'd take pictures tonight, like I had three nights in a row. Eventually either I'd find evidence, or the client would close the case because I couldn't find any. The estate file: I had to track down a missing heir. Something I could do online and in my Pjs.

The final one was the most interesting. Sara Lyman, missing wife. The cops had written her off as a runaway. She wasn't a kid and wasn't in a high-risk position to be murdered. People ran away all the time. I'd followed a money trail for a couple of days, and then the clues stopped. I needed to find another track. I was pretty sure there was more to it than a bad marriage. Maybe I could talk to her coworkers. I had that information scribbled on a scrap of notepaper.

So, far from having a heavy case load, I had a few hour's effort to close the cases. If I worked at it, I might be able to take a couple of days off.

I signed on to a few databases to put in some queries on the wife and the heir, turned on the coffee maker, and settled in for the afternoon.

Then someone knocked on my door.

It's not that easy to get to my door. I live in a floating home in Vancouver's Coal Harbour. Our little community of five floating homes was kept behind a security gate. Since I hadn't let anyone in through the gate, it could only be one of my neighbors, or Val, who never seemed to need a key or to be buzzed in.

I opened the door, hoping it wasn't Delores, the self-appointed neighborhood watch.

It was Iain. He lived in the last house on the finger dock, next to Jake's. He'd been there about six months. All I knew about him was that he had a friendly chocolate lab named Mickey and worked in some high-tech conglomerate. He looked the part. A little bit taller than me, and I'm tall for a woman at 5 feet 8 inches. A runner's body, but I've never seen him head off or return from a run. He'd be hard to pick out in a crowd because he's average. Brown hair, brown eyes, wears the not-quite-executive look; dark gray slacks white shirt and a dark blue tie. I guessed that he must be on a coffee break, or he goes in late to work.

"Hey, Charity," he said. Then nothing.

He'd obviously knocked for a reason, and now I was going to have to get it out of him. "Iain, is there something I can help you with?" Not original, but a gal has to keep things moving.

"Delores said you might help me."

He looked over my shoulder into my house, and I knew it would be faster if I invited him in so he could feel comfortable.

Thankful that I hadn't changed into my PJs yet, I opened

the door wider. "I have a few minutes, why don't you come inside."

He took one of the armchairs in my living room. Okay, I call it the living room, but it's more like a living area. Two chairs and a small couch sat around a coffee table, no room for anything else.

I waited a few minutes while Iain looked around him. I'd been in his house. It was smaller than mine, so he couldn't be feeling cramped.

He was going to be one of those clients. Some people know they need your help, but they are embarrassed, or feeling guilty, so they don't like to come out and state the facts.

"Delores thinks you need my help?" I prompted, but he just nodded. "I'm a private investigator, so you must need something investigated?"

He sighed, then straightened from his slouch and started to talk. "Mickey has been kidnapped. I guess I mean dognapped." He shook his head when I started to say I wasn't that kind of PI. "I know it's not a big case, but he's important to me. I need him back and I don't know what to do."

CHAPTER 2

He was almost in tears. I'm a sucker for a sad tale. I did not want to run around town looking for a lost dog, but maybe this dognapping would be more interesting than what I had on my plate. And how long could it take? "How do you know he's been taken? Maybe he just ran off and when he's bored, he'll come back."

Iain dug into his pocket and pulled out a wrinkled sheet of paper. "I got this stuffed into my mailbox."

It was a printout of a ransom note. Whoever had taken Mickey made it look like the letters came from newspaper clippings. Did they have a sense of humor? Or, didn't they know how to use a computer?

You want your dog back; we want five hundred bucks. If you don't pay the dog is never coming home.

Nothing else.

"Are you going to pay?"

He wiped his eyes, catching tears before they ran. There's a line between wimp and caring and Iain was getting close to the wimpy side of it. "I will, but they haven't told me where to go," he said.

"When did you get this?" I asked holding the note out.

"It was in my mailbox when I came home for lunch. So, ten minutes ago. Delores was there when I got it. I came right here."

If the dognappers were smart they would drop off another note or reach out some other way soon. They were asking a decent amount, something most people could afford if they had a dog. I had a feeling that Mickey wasn't their first victim.

"If you plan to pay, what do you want me to do?"

"I want you to find out who they are. I need Mickey back, and I don't want to wait. I can't take the risk that they'll take my money and keep him."

He'd lost his wimpy attitude. I got the feeling Mickey was more than just a pet.

I did not want to do this. It's not like I hate dogs, I just like humans better. Two missing people were waiting for my attention. If things went as I expected, Iain would get another note before the end of the day, and then he could pay the ransom. The problem is Iain's my neighbor, and if anything happened to his dog because I wouldn't help, I'd have to face that guilt every time I saw him.

Time for a compromise. "Do you have anything I can use as a clue? Like how they got Mickey in the first place?"

"He was in Dog Heaven. You know that spa on Georgia Street? When I got the note, I called. They said he'd been picked up by my brother. I don't have a brother. And I gave them an earful about their lack of security. Maybe they are in on it? You could start there."

Barging into a dog daycare and accusing the owners of a crime wasn't the best way to get information; especially if they called it a spa. But if I took the case, at least I had a lead. That was if I took the case. "Okay, Iain, here's the deal. I'm sure you'll get the instructions by the end of the day. Go get the cash.

When they call, come see me again. We'll figure out what to do."

He pushed himself up from the chair and reached out to shake my hand. "I feel better now with you on it. What's the fee?"

I hadn't taken the case, but I didn't want to argue it with him because I hadn't refused it either. "We'll talk fees when you hear from the dognappers. Maybe you won't need me."

I walked him the four steps to my door and watched him return to his house. I wasn't going to take on this case. I'd help him with paying the ransom and even with reporting the crime, but I had no time to track down anyone who kidnapped dogs for a living.

I WAS STILL FEELING KIND OF ANNOYED at Iain's request a couple of hours later. It was that kind of irritation that comes when someone asks you to do a favor, and says you can say no, but really the guilt at denying them is far more than the inconvenience of actually doing the favor. Then you get all mad that you feel guilty, and that they asked, and eventually you know you'll probably do it, but you have to stew for a while.

I'd set some searches going on the missing spouse and the lost heir. Most people who tried to disappear made some kind of mistake. I'd find a visa charge, or something that put me on the path. So, for the wife, I'd used both her married and maiden names. For the heir, I was pretty sure he wasn't trying to be lost. That one would be a matter of finding the one link that led to his door. When people disappeared and didn't get found... well it was more likely that they were dead than really good at hiding their tracks.

My phone buzzed as I got up to make a pot of coffee.

"Deacon Investigations." Maybe I'd change the name to

Deacon and Durand Investigations as a wedding present to Lu and Matthieu.

"I need someone who has experience with data loss." The voice was male, well spoken, no accent.

"That covers a lot. Can you give me more details?" Like a name? I usually didn't get the kind of client who kept things like that secret.

"Data security. That's all I can tell you right now."

Was this CISIS? CIA? NSA? Some other top secret, black ops organization? Probably just some small-time guy who lost a USB.

"Let's start with your name, then."

He sighed. "I said I can't tell you any details. Do you have experience with data loss?" Now he was pissed, and that seemed unwarranted.

"I don't work with anyone who doesn't trust me with his name."

"It's better that you don't know," he said. "Are you able to manage a case like this?"

Like what, asshole?

"Without details, I can't answer that question. If you have had a security breach, you need to contact someone with that expertise. I can give you some names."

"I don't want names. You come recommended."

"By who?" I really doubted that anyone I knew would recommend me for a data security job. I could set up some basic searches, and maybe hack through some simple features, but I wasn't a tech wiz.

"Can you help me?" He sounded desperate. Well, mad and desperate. That kind of client was more trouble than profit.

"No. Without details, I can't tell if we have the right skills. Would you like me to give you a few names that might be better suited?"

"So, you know enough to refer me, but you don't know enough to help me." He sneered the words.

Nasty.

"That's right. I'm sure you have more important things to do than argue with me." I wasn't going to waste any more of my time either. After all, I could be out dealing with dognappers.

He disconnected.

My irritation at Iain was gone. In its place was a gut twisting feeling that I should be afraid. Nothing the caller said was clearly menacing, but the whole call was off. I'd been threatened before, but never so oddly.

USE the QR code to grab a copy of AVARICE today.

FREE EBOOK

Claim your copy of Buying Into Death when you use the QR code to sign up for my newsletter and follow Charity as she solves her fastest case yet!

ALSO BY P A WILSON

For more books by P A Wilson

Use the QR code below or go to pawilson.ca

ABOUT THE AUTHOR

Perry Wilson is a Canadian author based in Vancouver, BC who has big ideas and an itch to tell stories. Having spent some time on university, a career, and life in general, she returned to writing in 2008 and hasn't looked back since (well, maybe a little, but only while parallel parking).

She is a member of the Vancouver Writers Social Group, The Royal City Literary Arts Society, and The Surrey Writing Workshop. Perry has self-published several novels. She writes the Madeline Journeys, a fantasy series about a high-powered lawyer who finds herself trapped in a magical world, the Quinn Larson Quests, which follows the adventures of a wizard named Quinn who must contend with volatile fae in the heart of Vancouver, and the Charity Deacon Investigations, a mystery thriller series about a private eye who tends to fall into serious trouble with her cases, and The Riverton Romances, a series based in a small town in Oregon, one of her favorite states. Her stand-alone novels are Breaking the Bonds, Closing the Circle, and The Dragon at The Edge of The Map.

For more information
www.pawilson.ca
pawilson@pawilson.ca

f X

ACKNOWLEDGMENTS

People think that the process of writing is solitary. That's not the case for me. I have help from so many people it would be hard to acknowledge everyone, but I'll give it a try.

The support and inspiration I get from my writer's groups is incalculable. The Vancouver Writers Social Group opens my mind to other ways of telling a story. The Royal City Literary Arts Society gives me the opportunity to meet and share with other writers who have more knowledge than I do. The Other 11 Months group is where I learn about getting the words on the page. And my critique group who helps me find the best parts of the story I want to tell. Thanks to all of the members of these great groups.

Last of all, but definitely a huge part of the process, my beta readers. These are the people who love stories and are willing, and more than able, to tell me if my finished story is ready for you, my readers.